Future Fiction

Edited by

Francesco Verso

Ecolution

Solarpunk Narratives
to Transform Reality

by Francesco Verso

Published by Associazione Future Fiction
Via Valentiniano 40 – 00145 Roma
TAX ID. 97962020588

Proofreading by Rachael Amoruso
Typesetting and formatting by Alda Teodorani.
Cover art illustration by Marzia Cardinale

Title: *Ecolution – Solarpunk Narratives to Transform Reality*
© 2024 Future Fiction, Roma
I edition July 2024
ISBN: 9788832077995
info@futurefiction.org

by Andrew Dana Hudson

This book isn't just a series of stories—it's a manual for thinking better about the future.

The solarpunk movement is now, in 2024 when I write this, a bit over ten years old. In that time, it's gone from a niche, hypothetical proposal for a fandom to a bustling literary genre, a recognizable aesthetic, and an ideological rallying point for countless activists and groups who desire a better, greener world. In 2023 the American progressive congresswoman Alexandria Ocasio-Cortez (AOC) called herself a solarpunk. Ten years from Tumblr posts to the literal halls of power—not a bad arc for a cultural project.

But one of the most extraordinary parts of the solarpunk story is how international it is. To tell that arc from American-owned social media network to American legislature is to tell but a sliver of the full tale. Solarpunk has often been *more* vibrant beyond the borders of our fading global hegemon, and much of that vibrancy is thanks to Francesco Verso.

In our present-day cyberpunk dystopia, there remain a few lingering borders, barriers between people that have not been ground into dust by networks and globalization and the logic of capital flows. Reading fiction written in another language remains out of reach even for us wired-up contemporary superhumans. Francesco has taken it upon himself to spread solarpunk beyond the anglophone world, beyond the confines of any one language. He's worked to bring English stories to Italian, Italian stories to Brazilian Portuguese, Brazilian stories to Mandarin Chinese—plus every other combination, and more.

His own stories (contained in this volume along with some of the clearest-eyed nonfiction writing about solarpunk you are likely to find) are similarly global in scope. They move from Italy to China to Siberia, with characters who feel entangled in the complexities of history and politics and the natural world. They are thoughtful stories about people who defy the hegemonic system, or who work for harmony with the *planetary* system, or both. And they are all, crucially, set *here*, on Earth, in futures built from the limitations and difficulties and promises of the present.

To me, that is the best kind of solarpunk: messy, angry, and hopeful all at once. These are the kind of stories we need to tell because these are the kind of stories we need to *live*. Solarpunk is a very different project than cyberpunk, one I like to call 'post-normal.' We aren't just trying to tell stories that entertain or that make sense of our present upheavals; we are trying to tell stories that help us change, to be new people building a better world. So don't just read these stories for the fun of it (though they are fun). Get out a pen and take some notes.

Andrew Dana Hudson
Tempe, Arizona, 2024

Solarpunk: New Seeds
from the Ashes of the Future

> We're *solarpunks* because the only other
> options are denial or despair.
> Adam Flynn

Mala tempora currunt, sed peiora parantur, this ancient complaint between the Latin and the vulgar, is enough to fully encapsulate the spirit of our times, or of those we have lived through at regular intervals. You only have to open a news site or watch the TV news for it to become clear how many tragedies and catastrophes are pummelling the human race on a daily basis: military conflicts and commercial wars, financial and economic failure, geopolitical tension and an ecological crisis caused by a production system increasingly hungry for fossil fuels with which it bankrolls its contradictory infinite development in a finite environment.

On the other hand, as William Gibson said in an interview in *Vulture* in 2017, updating the old adage where, "the future is already here—it is just not evenly distributed," "Dystopia is not very evenly distributed."[1]

Have these sensational narratives, constructed to generate paranoia and weekly apprehension, perhaps become the privilege of those who can afford to talk with a certain degree of arrogance about their self-indulgence? Or are they a pastime of a class with no empathy, whose level of humanity is being progressively reduced, moved, modelled?

---

1 Interview by Abraham Riesman with William Gibson. Vulture, 1 August, 2017 https://www.vulture.com/2017/08/william-gibson-archangel-apocalypses-dystopias.html.

Every kind of communication and entertainment, from films to books, comics and video games, does nothing other than ride on this long wave of stories that all look the same, metastasized narratives all pushing the same refrain on a global level, of a future tormented by totalitarianism and fundamentalism, global pandemics, zombie apocalypses, free-everyone superheroes, mutant trends and environmental disasters. It has already happened with the atomic bomb, the Cold War, Vietnam, the oil crisis, mad cow disease and the invasion of the "rogue states."

On the other hand, perhaps it is what happens when we subjugate our sensitiveness (and our nervous system) to entreaties that do not only come from other human beings and the external dynamics influencing their decision. "It is the phenomenon known as *automation bias* and it has been found in every sphere of computation, from spellcheck software to automatic pilots, and in every type of person. It is this prejudice that pushes us to consider automated information as more reliable than our own experiences, it appears unimportant if it conflicts with other observations, especially if these observations are ambiguous. Automated information is clear and direct and interferes with the grey areas that confuse our perception. Another phenomenon associated with this, *confirmation bias*, remodels our knowledge of the world to align it with automated information, confirming the validity of computerized solutions to the point of making us totally discard considerations that don't fit the machine's point of view."[2]

What will happen when we leave all the responsibility for writing—the news, drama, and dialogues between people

---

2 Kathleen Mosier, Linda Skitka, Susan Heers and Mark Burdick, "Automation Bias: Decision Making and Performance in High-Tech Cockpits," International Journal of Aviation Psychology 8:1, 1997, pag. 47-63.

and every narrative upon which we model our principles and according to which we prioritize things—to the algorithms and bots? The question doesn't even seem to be so linked to the narrative itself, rather more to its uniqueness and goals. However, it's "Not that such narratives are unneeded. At best, they can serve as a wake-up call for those caught up in the myth that we had reached the "end of history" with the fall of the Berlin Wall and the triumph of capitalism on a planetary scale. But if they remain the primary vision our globalised culture has of the potential future, they can end up reproducing the pervasive cynicism and despair which makes all crises seem inescapable."[3] Without taking into account that the new millennium has thrown us at supersonic speed into the era of post-everything: post-modern, post-apocalyptic, post-capitalist, post-truth, post-human, post-*.*, where the outlines of reality are more complex and elusive if not completely unfathomable, governed by forces we are beginning to notice only now, with what is perhaps guilty tardiness.[4]

For James Bridle the narratives of the present, with the momentum of the social networks, clickbait strategies, attention economy, and Big Data, have taken on even more threatening characteristics, "Just as global telecommunications have collapsed time and space, computing conflates the past with the future. That which is gathered as data is modelled as the way things are, and then projected forward—with the implicit assumption that things will not radically change nor diverge from previous experiences. In this way, computation does not merely govern our actions in the present, but it constructs a future that best fits its parameters. That which

---

3 From "What is solarpunk?" https://solarpunkanarchists.com/2016/05/27/what-is-solarpunk/.
4 From "What is solarpunk?" https://solarpunkanarchists.com/2016/05/27/what-is-solarpunk/.

is possible becomes that which is computable. That which is hard to quantify and difficult to model, that which has not been seen before or which does not map onto established patterns, that which is uncertain or ambiguous, is excluded from the field of possible futures. Computation projects a future that is like the past—which makes it, in turn, incapable of dealing with the reality of the present, which is, never stable.[5]

However, if we look closely, in every panorama devastated by the climate emergency, in every concrete jungle raised by global capitalism, something always grows. Not least because dystopia, catastrophism and fake news have become such frequent and normalized elements that they no longer raise the same sense of perturbation and marvel to be found in certain kinds of alternative narratives, like, for example, science fiction: is it still possible today to write and imagine something different to classic contemporary narratives? Is even just the hypothesis of a different economic system to capitalism a useless mental exercise without foundations or an almost nostalgic hippy or naive geek desire? Was Frederic Jameson right to affirm it is easier to imagine the end of the world than the end of capitalism? Is, in the light of current international policies on immigration, believing that the confines of nations can become porous to manage the climate emergency, an absurd idea only seasoned idealists can believe in? Or is it still possible to hope that as we passed from coal to oil, the same can happen with the sun, wind, and water? For decades, mainstream literature, in a progressive slide towards a disenchanted post-modernism and lucid cynicism justified by the crumbling of the present, has ably subtracted itself from the responsibility of imagining a different society, a different individual, and a future different from the current one.

---

5 James Bridle, New Dark Age, Verso Books, 2018.

"(...) [W]e ourselves are utterly enmeshed in techno-logical systems, which shape in turn how we act and how we think. We cannot stand outside them; we cannot think without them. Our technologies are complicit in the greatest challenges we face today: an out-of-control economic system that immiserates many and continues to widen the gap between rich and poor; the collapse of political and societal consensus across the globe resulting in increasing national-isms, social divisions, ethnic conflicts and shadow wars; and a warming climate, which existentially threatens us all."[6]

Therefore, where can we look for other possible worlds and alternative solutions to the usual representation of a present that is incapable of renewing itself? Other coloniz-able worlds? In the malleable folds of the deepest space? Or in a time *uchronically* consolatory or perhaps so far off to be, by definition, hardly plausible?

Science fiction, whose stories are, by nature, transforma-tion narratives, has the ambition of describing what does not exist, at least not yet, but in certain conditions might occur. Therefore, writers of this genre present themselves as excellent world builders, proposing future studies of a tomorrow with hazy, elusive outlines. Since science fiction lives in the future, it knows the value (made of trends, po-tential and hope) and the defects (clearly wrong conjecture, the prophetic unreality of "Cassandra syndrome" and "cry-wolf" alarmism, which many narratives fall down on). How-ever, after having destroyed the world thousands of times over, after having celebrated its suffered rebirth and having hypothesized the most bizarre but impossible Utopias, pass-ing through post-human transformations, technocratic drifts and bio-political transformations, we find emerging—from more than one part of the world and the most disparate areas

---

6 James Bridle, New Dark Age, Verso Books, 2018, pag. 10.

of knowledge—a small nucleus of *solarpunk* stories that set out to challenge the ineluctable solidity of the present.

In such a turbulent period—when the global narrative is obstinately centred on decadence, cynicism, and dystopia—there are people who are devoted to delineating the outline of "another world." In practice it has been, until now, a series of stories, illustrations, essays and discussions on social media and the online communities, even though many see solarpunk as the start of something bigger, something that could distance us from contemporary dissatisfaction. It is a minor, almost latent trend, which is often accused of being nothing more than a flight of fancy, the inconclusive desire for a perfect society even though, in reality, things are more complex: utopianism is the life force of change, it is the sand that gets caught in the cogs of the status quo and has, over the centuries, never stopped inspiring people and movements with the aim of improving the human condition.

Just look at Galileo Galilei, Martin Luther King, the suffragettes, Vandana Shiva and Aaron Swartz. Or, to return to science fiction: Edward Bellamy, Ursula Le Guin, Iain Banks, Octavia Butler and Kim Stanley Robinson.

It is not by chance that science fiction was the first to gather the seeds of this change in perspective. As with *climate fiction*, the narrative about climatic changes: since science fiction considers reality to be inadequate, devoid of those imaginary elements that complete human life, it criticises apparent reality, it presupposes that things might go in a different manner and speculates creatively about the future without worrying about the vice-like grip of the present. Indeed, it leap-frogs over it as the obstacle to free imagination that it is.

Solarpunk is therefore a reaction to the cynicism and pessimism in visions of the near future. Naturally, cynicism and pessimism cannot be replaced by blind, ingenuous, infantile optimism, but by a cautious hope, and audaciousness to focus on the potential to be found even in the most difficult of situations. No dramatist worthy of the name can disregard a conflict or distance themselves from a questioning of their actual reality and identity, so to get back to the aforementioned narratives, what really is their aim, the message they want to transmit? Perhaps, if we try to cultivate these seeds, something more ecological, liberating and egalitarian could rise from the legacy the Post*.* are leaving us.

As often happens, it is the young people who carry these seeds in their hands. In the words of Greta Thunberg, a Swedish sixteen-year-old, at the COP24 in Katowice, "You only speak of green eternal economic growth because you are too scared of being unpopular. You only talk about moving forward with the same bad ideas that got us into this mess, even when the only sensible thing to do is pull the emergency brake. You are not mature enough to tell it like it is. Even that burden you leave to us children. (...) You say you love your children above all else, and yet you are stealing their future in front of their very eyes. Until you start focusing on what needs to be done rather than what is politically possible, there is no hope. We cannot solve a crisis without treating it as a crisis. We need to keep the fossil fuels in the ground, and we need to focus on equity. And if solutions within the system are so impossible to find, maybe we should change the system itself. We have not come here to beg world leaders to care. You have ignored us in the past and you will ignore us again. We have run out of excuses and we are running out of time. We have come here to let you know that change is coming, whether you like it or not. The real power belongs to the people. Thank you."[7]

---

7 Thunburg Citation

If all the alarms have already gone off, the horses have escaped, the dystopian trend has been reported and if every apocalypse has ended in an even worse one without anyone doing anything, then either we really are finished, or it is worth changing the narrative (to change direction). At least it is for people who don't kid themselves that words are enough to put out the fire spreading across the world. This is not even a metaphor. "In 2015, for the first time in at least 800,000 years the atmospheric carbon dioxide passed 400 ppm. At its current rate, which shows no signs of abating, and we show no sign of stopping, atmospheric $CO2$ will have reached ,000 ppm by the end of the century. At 1,000 ppm, human cognitive ability drops by 21 percent. At higher atmospheric concentrations $CO2$ stops us from thinking clearly."[8,9]

Welcome to the Anthropocene.

Solarpunk, energy from above, action from below.

The first trace of solarpunk stories appeared in Brazil with the publication of *Solarpunk*: *Histórias ecológicas e fantásticas emum mundo sustentável* edited by Gerson Lodi-Riberio (Draco, 2012), then translated by Fabio Fernandes into English and published as *Solarpunk: Ecological and Fantastical Stories in a Sustainable World* (World Weaver Press, 2018). Meanwhile, in 2014, Adam Flynn wrote a brief, but fundamental article entitled, *Solarpunk: Notes Toward a Manifesto*. Following this, further anthologies of stories like *Sunvault: Stories of Solar-*

---

8 Joseph G. Allen, et al. "Associations of Cognitive Function Scores with Carbon Dioxide, Ventilation, and Volatile Organic Compound Exposures in Office Workers: A Controlled Exposure Study of Green and Conventional Office Environments," Environmental Health Perspectives 124, June 2016, pag. 805-12.
9 James Bridle, New Dark Age, Verso Books, 2018, pag. 87.

punk and Eco-Speculation, edited by Phoebe Wagner and Brontë Christopher Wieland (Upper Rubber Boot, 2017); *Eco-Punk, Speculative Tales of Radical Futures*, edited by Liz Grzyb and Cat Sparks (Ticonderoga Publications, 2017); and *Glass and Gardens: Solarpunk Summers*, edited by Sarena Ulibarri (World Weaver Press, 2018). We must also remember two precursors of solarpunk in the margins, the films of Hayao Miyazaki so far as regards aesthetics and political challenges (above all *Princess Mononoke*), and the novel by Ernest Callenbach, *Ecotopia: The Notebooks and Reports of William Weston* from 1975, in which an anti-capitalist, de-urbanized society centred around gardens is envisaged.

The term solarpunk became popular on Tumblr in 2014 as a reaction to an image gallery that caught the attention of a large number of bloggers and developed on sites like *solapunkanarchist.com* and *medium.com/solarpunk,* giving rise to series of posts and thoughts ranging from circular economy to environmental sustainability, from criticizing predatory capitalism to creating off-grid networks, from the use of renewable resources to resilient communities fighting against gentrification, even going as far as the aesthetics of Art Nouveau, and fashion that reworks the canons of African and Asian art in modern terms, and touching on bio camouflage/mimicry: the imitation of shapes and organic functions with the aim of improving products and experiences, and the Anthropocene, meant this time as the geological era brought on by human behavior.

For Andrew Dana Hudson, an activist in the movement and author of essays and stories about the genre, solarpunk is a "*speculative movement*: a collaborative effort to imagine and design a world of prosperity, peace, sustainability and beauty, achievable with what we have from where we are."[10] According to Adam Flynn, solarpunk "envisions stories set in a future that runs on renewable energy, such as solar or wind, and where race- or gender-based discrimination is more limited than it is today. . . . Its aesthetic is solar panels, windmills, and leafy, high-tech societies."[11]

Contrary to steampunk, which intentionally takes refuge in a nostalgic romanticism from the Victorian era thereby deflecting from technological realism, and cyberpunk, which has both denounced the ascent of the technocracy, and the class fight between rich capitalists of the kind Yuval Noah Harari defines as "Dataism"[12] and poor geeks and nerds exploited without ever finding solutions, solarpunk explores exit strategies from the actual socio-economic situation through plausible and pragmatic narratives that for the first time reply to the Anthropocene in a conscious and constructive way, a *hyper-project*, as Timothy Morton calls it in the book of the same name, the real features of which we have only recently come to notice.[13]

---

10 Andrew Dana Hudson, https://medium.com/solarpunks/on-the-political-dimensions-of-solarpunk-c5a7b4bf8df4.
11 Interview with Adam Flynn, https://www.ozy.com/fast-forward/sci-fi-doesnt-have-to-be-depressing-welcome-to-solarpunk/82586.
12 Yuval Noha Harari, Homo Deus: A Brief History of Tomorrow, Perennial, 2016.
13 Timothy Morton, Hyperobjects, University of Minnesota Press, 2013.

In political terms, solarpunk tends to distinguish itself from the false dichotomy that has the market economy on one side and state socialism on the other, between individualism pushed to extreme competition and suffocating collectivism; a hypothetical solarpunk society should rely on the healthy development of people within a supportive community, which also relies on long-term renewable energy. Utopia? Perhaps, even though the goal to reach is not perfection in itself (it is enough to remember that a dictator's utopia is everyone else's dystopia), but to move, constant and progressive, towards certain ideals. Even though solarpunk realizes that many objectives (social justice, fair distribution of profits and environmental sustainability, just to mention some of the "north stars" to follow) might never be achieved, this awareness does not diminish its relevance and originality, nor how it combats the effects of roughly two hundred years of capitalism.

Ideally, solarpunk continues the fight of cyberpunk against the economic power of the multinationals and the authority of the state, but above all it concentrates on going against any attempt at subjugating the human race to forces that have very little humanity in them, like financial speculation, environmental externalization, predictive algorithms, the privatization of public property and services, the prejudicial filters of artificial intelligences and measures that taste of biopolitical law. It encompasses everything that is the movement against the control and management of human beings, what Jochi Ito calls "Resisting Reduction" (MIT Press, 2019). However, this "punk" opposition, which often takes on aspects of civil disobedience, draws momentum from the semantic root of its name, "solar" implying positivity, solidarity and democracy (the sun shines on everybody, without distinction). In Hudson's words, "I see solarpunk emerging as a reaction to this sensation of strangling decay.

People want to feel the vibrancy of progress, not just the anxious giddiness of capitalist churn. We want to seek out and apply our true talents, not warp our lives around making money for other, richer people. We want our work to mean something more than survival."

Therefore, if on one side cyberpunk prefigured the socio-political dynamics of the present through the "low-life/hi-tech" paradigm (Mark Zuckerberg selling people's personal data to multinationals is celebrated as a captain of industry and his "bad actions"—at most, cause for a fine for privacy violation—whereas Julian Assange, who leaked the secrets of multinationals into the public domain, is arrested as a criminal, just to cite two examples of cyberpunk in real life), on the other side we have solarpunk preparing the field for the imaginary collective of the next thirty or forty years, inverting the terms of the paradigm and upending the metaphor into "hi-energy/low-act" (energy from above, action from below). Adam Flynn, writer on the Project Hieroglyph blog of *Solarpunk: Notes Toward a Manifesto,* said "The great programs of the 20th century often began as fictional proposals, from moon landings to Social Security. It's time we returned to higher ambitions for what we can do as a society."

The time seems ripe if we consider the struggle against global warming (kids skipping school on *Fridays for Future,* the civil disobedience movement *Extinction Rebellion* and the search for off-grid energy independence solutions), the production of goods from the bottom up (3D printing digital craftspeople and the local produce economy), free access to data (Open Access and mesh networks) or new kinds of social interaction (tiny-houses, resilient communities and Strong Towns) and the mutual help networks (Occupy Sandy, We're the 99%) as agents of transformation and signals of change.

From the ashes of steampunk and cyberpunk.
If we use the models of Koert van Mensvoort, inspired by the Maslow need pyramid, to represent technological innovations and social changes it is possible to trace the progress of any transformation through the 7 levels of development.[14]

To start with, all technology must be envisioned (meaning it comes from an idea, a dream or a vision, like, for example, the theory of relativity, or 3D printing); then, it becomes operational (through prototypes or experiments like meat grown in vitro); then, it is applied and becomes accessible to a number of people (as it comes out of the laboratories, as with Google Glasses); and then, stepping up a level, its use becomes accepted on a large scale (that is, it becomes part of our daily life as in the case of smartphones) and filters through every level of the population, becoming an element without which we would find it difficult to live (internet, the sewage system), to the point of becoming a vital part of the tissue of reality (taking on natural characteristics and becoming almost indistinguishable from any other element considered natural, like agriculture and writing).

---

14 From the website Next Nature, https://www.nextnature.net/2014/08/pyramid-of-technology/.

However, alongside the vertical axis of development we also have to consider the horizontal axis of time and progressive ageing, or technological obsolescence, of any innovation, whether it is technical, social, or political. After a certain period, after, that is, any "novum"—to use a term so dear to Darko Suvin—has produced its effect of "cognitive estrangement," introducing an element into a familiar but such a diverse reality as to cause fear (if negative) and wonder (if positive), this is when the experience of such changes no longer creates any strong feelings within us, no longer incites our curiosity, no longer disturbs us to the point of fearing it, because it has become a normality, the standard we have learned to recognize. Then all innovations and social transformations introduced by that novum stop producing the original sense of wonder, that sense of awe and desire to discover, which is the foundation of the science fiction narrative.

Here is a concrete example: imagine you are reading a story where the main character is a woman who can live her sexual relationships without anxiety because she is taking a hormone pill capable of reducing the possibility of falling pregnant to almost zero, like magic and without any physical consequences. What would be the reaction of a woman reading this story before the 1900s? She would certainly take it for science fiction. To someone reading it in the 1960s? Perhaps she would be fearful, scared, but who knows, maybe she would try it like many women of the era did. A reader from today? It would probably be difficult for her to do without.

This is why I define science fiction as anything capable of making reality obsolete from a technological, social, or political standpoint. After the invention of the (contraceptive) pill nothing was the same again: couples' relationships, birth control, family rights and society transformed in a libertarian sense, suddenly deleting the preceding history and giving women complete control over the decision process. Contraceptive methods existed before the pill, but its almost absolute effectiveness, and the fact that control was suddenly in the hands of the woman, made it an unparalleled tool of transformation.

Does this mean only technology and changes still in the stages of discovery and new application can create the desire or anxiety to understand what would happen if that novum became reality?

Steampunk is the perfect opposite example. In its imagined, anachronistic technology, by resorting to already familiar, two-century-old aesthetics from steam engines and electrical energy to lace and velvet from the Victorian age, it uses a worn-out novum as a broken arrow, filling the narrative with weapons loaded with blanks. This can make an excellent story with well-turned characters but cannot open roads of new knowledge in a reader, nor generate a true sense of the wonderful because of its lack of an alienating element. Paradoxically, if it did it would be science fiction! Instead of asking "what would happen if?", steampunk and fantasy already provide the answer. It's a pity that the question, by becoming "how good would the world have been if…," makes any reality implode and the narration escapist and, at best, consolatory.

Cyberpunk is different, its novels are almost always set in strongly anthropized glass and concrete megalopolises, in endless panoramas like William Gibson's horizontal "sprawl" in *Neuromancer* and Ridley Scott's dark, vertical Los Angeles in *Blade Runner*, non-places where natural experiences are sold at high prices in the form of vegetation furnishings, animatronic pets and virtual realities. In these panoramas, subjected to the turbo-capitalism that barters the mirage of wealth for the illusion of security, man doesn't live, he survives, avoiding pollution and contamination, withdrawing into dark, protected spaces and hermetically isolated from any external contact, whether physical, social or emotive. The hero of a cyberpunk story is, typically, like Case, the virtual network cowboy, protagonist of *Neuromancer*, a solitary individual, white and American, a social misfit who manages by exploiting his one talent: programming.

Cyberpunk's denouement of technocrat globalization, urban alienation and IT criminality doesn't find solutions except in partial victories by single individuals, a momentary salvation by the hacker, until the next battle, until the next stop in this interminable journey at the end of existential precariousness.

Exactly where we are now. The "zero degree, the dark present where we understand nothing beyond movement and efficiency, and where the only action we are allowed is to accelerate the existing order."[15]

After adding it all up, if steampunk tells stories of retro-futures where (nostalgically) we would have liked to have lived and cyberpunk tells of a future present already (cynically) created where we wouldn't like living, solarpunk, on the other hand, prefigures environments where (pragmatically) we might like to live, if we roll up our sleeves.

In solarpunk, whether the individual or a group, the main characters don't give up on the fight for repossession of capitalism's abandoned spaces or state inefficiency. This transforms into a fight in the name of human necessity, a principle shared by the community, the neighborhood or a whole country against gentrification, expropriation, abuse of and the loss of identity.

In the article "On the Need for New Futures," Adam Flynn says these stories focus on "finding ways to make life more wonderful for us right now, and more importantly for the generations that follow us—i.e., extending human life at the species level, rather than individually. Our future must

---

15 James Bridle, New Dark Age, Verso Books, 2018.

involve repurposing and creating new things from what we already have (instead of 20th century "destroy it all and build something completely different" modernism). Our futurism is not nihilistic like cyberpunk and it avoids steampunk's potentially quasi-reactionary tendencies: it is about **ingenuity, generativity, independence, and community."**

From essays and stories published up until now, it is possible to construct a parallel between cyberpunk and solarpunk starting from key elements as shown in the following diagram.

CYBERPUNK - DYSTOPIA	SOLARPUNK - UTOPIA
Capitalism: Bankarchy, Private property, Multinationals, Classism, Speculation, Globalization and work automation, High profits/low salaries, Competition.	Anticapitalism Blockchain, Creative Commons, Mass co-operation, P2P economy, Crowdfunding, Crowdsourcing, Social equity, Non-profit, Reciprocal aid.
Mass industry: Fossil fuels, Negative externality, Big Pharma, Agrobusiness, GDP index.	Circular economy: Renewable resources, Recycling, Permaculture, Human Development Index.
Urbanization: E-waste, Deregulation, Gentrification, Brutalism, Bio-political architecture	Deurbanization: Resilient communities, Mini-homes, Urban kitchen gardens, Local produce, Bioarchitecture.
Info-tech Virtual reality, Networks and Computers, Databases, Biotechnology, Synthetic drugs.	Biomimicry: Artificial photosynthesis, Social Networks, 3D printing, A.I., Nanotechnology.

Andrew Dana Hudson, in his essay "On the Political Dimensions of Solarpunk" explains, "Solarpunk should move quietly and plant things. Don't ask permission from a state beholden to oligarchs, and definitely don't expect those oligarchs to do any of this for you. Guerilla gardening is the model, but look further. Guerilla solar panel installation. Guerilla water treatment facility restoration. Guerilla magnificent temple to the human spirit construction. Guerilla carbon sequestration megastructure creation."

In this way the fight of the individual or of the few, becomes the fight of many. Who fights for an idea instead of for their own benefit often finds allies along the way.

More than a genre, less than an ideology.
Technological innovation, on its own, does not guarantee any sociopolitical improvement. Transformations are always accompanied by modifications to the cultural and psychological sphere, altering people's choices and therefore their behavior.

The story of solar energy is proof. The first to use it, building houses oriented along a north-south axis to maximize exposure to the sun's rays in the winter, were the Greeks, who did this because of the lack of firewood on their land. It was the ancient Romans, though, who used it on a large scale for both domestic heating and in grandiose architectural projects like the Baths of Diocletian. They even included the right to solar exposition for their famous helio-fireplaces, which heated houses, in the corpus of the ***Codex Justinianeus***.

Since then and for the whole of the Middle Ages, solar power more or less disappeared until after enlightenment. "In the eighteenth and early nineteenth centuries, innovations in solar architecture saw a major boom. Spurred by the

"Little Ice Age" spanning from 1550 to 1850—a geological oddity in which Europe went through an extremely cold period—alternate heating methods led to the proliferation of glass-cased structures and the "Age of the Greenhouse" . . . The ability to cultivate produce year-round was especially desirable given the new imported colonial fruits Europeans had developed a taste for."[16]

With the growing of the middle classes, glasshouses gave way to conservatories, rooms with solar heating where instead of agricultural produce, wonders of the botanical world were displayed as if they were valuable objects and marks of wealth, to the point that they became an important feature of late Victorian architecture. A century later, when the use of coal was widespread, the conservatories were no longer heated with the sun's natural energy but artificially, with fossil fuels. At the start of the 1900s, with the arrival of Art Nouveau, the glasshouses had already lost their original function and became simple ornaments inspired by nature, a decorative example of sustainable architecture, demoted to a form of permitted pastime for housewives.

Amongst the first to use solar technology in modern times, we must remember Augustin Mouchot: the French mathematician who invented a solar powered steam engine prototype in about 1860. Hailed as a wonder, he was sent to Algeria because the French sun was not strong enough to power the machine. Once there, Mouchot developed other designs including solar powered cookers and water purification devices, however, the rapid improvement of coal extraction techniques and transport soon put an end to a premature "Solar Age" which still, despite appropriate technology having been

____

16 Elvia Wilk, "Is Ornamenting Solar Panels a Crime?" e-flux, https://www.e-flux.com/architecture/positions/191258/is-ornamenting-solar-panels-a-crime/.

ready for years, does not seem to be arriving with the necessary determination due to the lack of political and industrial enthusiasm towards a transition to natural energy.

Aesthetically, solarpunk brings nature back to the center and observes it attentively and differently to how it has been viewed recently, with artificial materials and a post-modern flavor. We are not talking about floral fantasies or a return to a sort of "primitivism." On the contrary, biomimicry, drawing inspiration from and using materials, designs and models inspired by nature, provides for the insertion or fusion of these elements in urban infrastructures, in public and private buildings, and even in the fabrics clothes are made of.

Augustin Mouchot's solar engine on display at the 1878 Paris Universal Exhibition.

Instead of mimicking nature with artificial tools, nature's natural processes are imitated: just think, for example, of solar geoengineering, also known as solar radiation management, to fight global warming by releasing large quantities of sulphuric acid into the atmosphere (at about 20 km from the Earth's surface) to reflect and disperse a portion of sunlight into space.[17,18] This gentle shading, by reducing the quantity of solar energy reaching the planet, will reduce the effects of global warming caused by greenhouse gases like carbon dioxide, mitigating, at least partially, the general situation. Just think about the dream of artificial photosynthesis proposed for the first time by the Italian chemist Giacomo Ciamician during the eighth International Applied Chemistry Congress in New York on September 11, 1912. Talking about "The Photochemistry of the Future," Ciamician indicated the road to follow with words that still sound prophetic today, "the future of chemistry and industry, . . . is clear: it all lies with our ability to learn to 'work like plants,' meaning the ability to transform sunlight (radiation energy) into the ordered movement of electrons (biochemical energy) and save this energy in complex molecules. Put in other words, we chemists have to learn how photosynthesis works. The future, not only and not particularly of chemistry, but also and mostly of humanity, will greatly depend on our ability to develop artificial photosynthesis."[19]

The main obstacle in the path of the development of artificial photosynthesis is that in nature the process is inefficient. Plants only convert the minimum necessary for survival, roughly 1% of the carbon and water in carbohydrates. However, efficiency reached in the lab has reached

---

17 Image below from https://designgallerist.com/blog/garden-rhapsody-beautiful-experience-music-lights/.

18 Image below from https://materialdistrict.com/article/seeing-unseen/seeing-the-unseen-3/.

19 "Lavorare per il sogno di Ciamician," Micron, July 20, 2019, https://www.rivistamicron.it/temi/lavorare-per-il-sogno-di-ciamician/.

roughly 10% and recently researchers at Monash University in Melbourne, Australia, reached an efficiency level of 22%.

Moving onto another important aspect of the solarpunk approach, in an answer to a question from Suzanne Jacobs about the design idea of the movement, Adam Flynn replied, "We need to think about a design paradigm . . . a little bit more built-to-last and modular, able to be adapted to events in the future that we can't foresee. Things like Rails-to-Trails I really love because it's the clever adaptation of existing infrastructure toward things that benefit us in the here and now, so that we don't have these giant mega-projects gathering dust somewhere because the assumptions that undergirded it are no longer tenable. Eventually, it would be really nice if we had one of those modular smartphone things, where you just replace things bit by bit.[20] I'm generally on the side of the people who think you should be able to open and repair your technology. As beautiful as the experience of Apple's walled garden has been, it's encouraged a sense of opacity and passivity towards our technology that I think is regrettable."[21]

Solarpunk, in keeping with the idea of radical inclusiveness, fuses the solar architecture of ancient peoples with the futuristic visions of architects such as Paolo Soleri and his prototype of arcology called *arcosanti* in Arizona, the bioarchitecture of Vincent Callebaut and Stefano Boeri, who is currently occupied in the construction of a Forest City, an urban model of environmental regeneration, energy sustain-

---

20 Rails to Trails are public multi-use trails built on disused railroad corridors, https://www.railstotrails.org/.
21 Interview with Adam Flynn, https://grist.org/business-technology/this-sci-fi-enthusiast-wants-to-make-solarpunk-happen/.

ability and increased biodiversity in Liuzhou in southern China, despite the risks of turning it into a pure ecomodernist project available only for very rich people.

In an attempt to create artistic cross-pollination, solarpunk brings together suggestions from the most diverse sources, from cutting-edge technology from the Maker Fair, artistic avant-garde from Afrofuturism and flashes of counter-culture from the Burning Man Festival, to remodel them into something liberating, reworking and reinventing styles and trends in a different context. It is a transversal hybridization celebrating popular antique wisdom as a conversation about our identity, craftsmen's experience against mass production of objects and alienating experiences, respect for cultural diversity and integrated technological development—something creative and sustainable, while still remaining sensitive to the problems of cultural appropriation, the "taking" instead of "participating" typical of dominant cultures towards the subordinate ones.

One of the biggest risks is the normalization of the revolutionary content of solarpunk: to be reduced to a meme, a trend, a hashtag, put on the shelves as a shiny cover or worn by a smiling model and displayed in the window and sold like the dream of a shiny future.

"A snappy label and a manifesto," said William Gibson in an interview in the Paris Review in 2011, "would have been two of the very last things on my own career want list. That label enabled mainstream science fiction to safely assimilate our dissident influence, such as it was. Cyberpunk could then be embraced and given prizes and patted on the head, and genre science fiction could continue unchanged. . . I didn't have a manifesto. I had some discontent. It seemed to me that mid-century mainstream American science fiction had often been triumphalist and militaristic, a sort of folk propaganda for American exceptionalism. I was tired of America-as-the-future, the world as a white monoculture, the protagonist as a good guy from the middle class or above. I wanted there to be more elbow room. I wanted to make room for antiheroes."[22]

Shrimp fishers next to solar panels in a solar-solar hydroelectric power plant in Yangzhou, China (VCG) via @justinpickard

As has already happened with cyberpunk, the danger is that solarpunk could be reduced to another passing fashion, absorbed by consumerism and transformed into just another entertainment tool for mass distraction. On the contrary, solarpunk is like a container of narratives countering the hypotheses, present and future, that preclude the construction of valid alternatives.

---

22 "William Gibson, The Art of Fiction No. 211," The Paris Review, 2011, https://www.theparisreview.org/interviews/6089/william-gibson-the-art-of-fiction-no-211-william-gibson.

The two souls of the phenomenon: Solar + Punk

Composed of the root "solar" and the suffix "punk," solarpunk gathers elements that at first glance may seem far apart, if not actually contradictory. However, upon closer analysis, it is not hard for them to coexist. The use solarpunk narratives make of the two terms can be represented in this table outlining the main principles.

As ambitious as Solarpunk's objectives might appear, they are not so far away from the goals of most countries' constitutions, "A solarpunk culture would strive to dissolve every form of social hierarchy and domination—whether based on class, race, gender, sexuality, ability, or species—dispersing the power some individuals or groups wield over others and thus increasing the aggregate freedom of all; empowering the disempowered and including the excluded. It is rooted in the legacy of such liberatory movements as anti-authoritarian socialism, feminism, racial justice, queer and trans liberation, disability struggles, animal liberation, and digital freedom projects."[23]

In shattering the rigidity with which mainstream narratives describe the present, between the infinite growth of capitalism and the apocalyptic catastrophe of its detractors, solarpunk follows its tortuous and potholed path towards a change perceived by many as necessary. Even if it is neither possible nor desirable to create perfect worlds, this does not mean we should be scared to imagine a better future, especially when the fight against inequality and environmental pollution are within our reach. Whether this is in the form of a science fiction narrative, technological innovation, a civil movement or a political party, solarpunk is the toolbox with which to build a better tomorrow.

---

23 From the article "What is Solarpunk?" https://solarpunkanarchists. com/2016/05/27/what--solarpunk/.

Solar	Punk
Light: countering the darker more decadent tones of current science fiction and narratives about the present in global media.	**Rebellion:** exploration of everything that goes against the system, the hunt for "other" solutions, not necessarily negative, criticism and discussion of reality.
Day: countering the permanent night of cyberpunk and dystopian stories.	**Counterculture:** where our culture is pessimistic and anthropocentric, the counterculture can be hopeful and mutually beneficial. Rejection of mass consumerism, choosing do-it-yourself.
Solar	Punk
Clean energy: as an instrument for not damaging the environment and ourselves. The union of nature and technology against the subjugation of the Earth through deforestation, pollution and heavy industry.	**Enthusiasm:** The positive energy of a rock concert or of a Maker Fair. Attaining objectives with that contagious energy source of continual inspiration.
Inclusion of marginalized groups: In the same way the sun touches everybody uncaring of race and class, it is necessary to include whoever has a physical or mental disability, ethnic minorities and people discriminated against for their political or sexual preferences.	**Tribalism:** Aesthetics and group identity made up of leather clothing, tattoos, piercing, Mohawks and shaved heads to recognize each other and to create a sense of belonging and community from which a new sensitivity can emerge.

As Oscar Wilde said, "A map of the world that does not include Utopia is not worth even glancing at, for it leaves out the one country at which Humanity is always landing. And when Humanity lands there, it looks out, and, seeing a better country, sets sail. Progress is the realisation of Utopias."[24]

To conclude, "The technologies that so inform and shape our contemporary perceptions of reality are not going to go away, and in many cases, we should not wish them to. Our current life-support systems on a planet of 7.5 billion and rising, utterly depend upon them. Our understanding of those systems and their ramifications and of the conscious choices we make in their design remain entirely within our capabilities. We are not powerless, not without agency, and not limited by darkness. We only have to think, and think again, and keep thinking. The network—us and our machines and the things we think and discover together—demand it."[25]

If science fiction helps us to reflect on the future, solarpunk proposes solid strategies for creating a desirable one, now, wherever we are and with what we have, for us and for the generations following us. Hopefully it won't be yet another false start.

---

24 Oscar Wilde, "The Soul of Man Under Socialism," 1891.
25 James Bridle, New Dark Age, Verso Books, 2018, pag. 281.

*Ma noi vogliamo convivere con i regali
della natura o vogliamo distruggerli per com-
prarci non si sa bene cosa? Perché cambia a
ogni stagione.*
Chiara Vigo

THE DENIAL

The bank's revolving door spits her out like rotten food.

Carla mouths "Fuck you" at the clerk who shakes his head on the other side of the glass. Then she grimaces and sticks her tongue out at the uniformed security android manning the guard's cabin. The guard's eyes emit a sequence of flickering red light and he moves to stand up, but the clerk motions him to stay put. Carla yanks open the security locker at the entrance, slamming the door to make a point, and snatches back her rings, chains and the cell phone to call her safety anchor.

"Hello Basma, yes, it didn't go well," she says as soon as she gets the earbuds in, outside the Ostiense/Garbatella branch of the bank.

"What happened this time?"

The traffic has been blocked by a self-driving car that has lost its GPS signal and is circling the roundabout over and over again. A cacophony of car horns rips through the air, and, as if this wasn't enough, the sun is beating down so strongly on Carla's head she has to shield her eyes with her other hand, as she heads towards her bicycle leaning against the wall of the nearby school.

"The usual thing... First, he checked the damn credit rating database and found the notes about our three previous requests that were all denied."

She wants to rip the bike chain apart, kick it, and twist it around the clerk's neck; instead, she taps in the lock's combination on her phone.

"But they weren't seriously bad. . . just a bit late," Basma answers. "We paid off the lapsed installments, it's been more than a year."

"Exactly, then he saw the last five years of zero-hour contracts."

"The bastard. . ."

Carla's t-shirt is sticking to her back, leaving large sweat rings on it.

"And he kept raising his eyebrows with an air of superiority, then I lost it."

"What did you do, Carla? You didn't hit him, did you?"

"I held back, but I did tell him we needed the money to install two Kuka arms in the Fab Lab to print low-cost medical prostheses, not for buying drugs, like his disgusted expression said he thought we wanted it for."

Having unlocked her bike, Carla jumps on it and pushes herself onto the road.

"Did he at least look at our business plan with the prototypes and applications?"

"Yes, he glanced at the pictures, like everyone else before him, and he just didn't get it, exactly like everyone else before him. In the end, do you know what he came up with?"

As soon as her cell low battery warning beeps, Carla unwinds a USB cable from her backpack and connects it to a tulip wind turbine socket whizzing around busily on the handlebars.

"That banks need guarantees, even with the remotest possibility of non-fulfillment, blah blah blah, and therefore without guarantees, a house would have been useful."

"I hope you didn't offer up the farmhouse."

"Of course not, that's when I got up and flipped him the bird, doubled."

The traffic moves in stops and starts along Via Ostiense while she speeds along the emergency lane and the footpath in an attempt to avoid the piles of rubbish that threaten to make her fall every few hundred meters.

"Then, like he was offended, he added that our occupied house—albeit in dilapidated conditions and in the remote hypothesis of sale—might not be enough to cover our request for 25,000 euro."

Usually, in the proximity of videolights showing red, Carla prefers to zigzag through the lines of traffic for two reasons: 1) it's still faster than the cars controlled by the proximity sensors at the intersectionit's fun to taunt the people steaming in their self-propelled tins.

"What are you doing now?"

"Coming back home, what else?"

"Remember your sun cream! The sun is ferocious today."

"Yes, mummykins," she answers, grabbing a tube from the pocket of her fanny pack. Pulling off the lid with her teeth, she squeezes two stripes of cream over her shoulders. "How I wish this stuff could turn some heat into energy and not just sweat."

"Maybe somebody is already working on it."

Burning with rage, Carla settles the mask on her face and pushes harder on the pedals. The tulips are humming in a pleasant and energizing way, like lots of little turbines.

THE RETURN

Serra Spino covers an entire hill just beyond the beltway, at the end of Via Portuense. Carla has been living there as a squatter for three years with the friends she took over the abandoned farmhouse with. It had been an old ruin on land belonging to a farm that supplied Torre in Pietra dairy with milk. In the distance, the rounded silhouettes of the Building Composites to country road to dusty, dirt track. Her bike bucks between the holes, bumps and tree roots in the cracked pavement.

Today the pickets protesting against the Malagrotta dump aren't out. The line of cars resigned to being in a jam usually stretches all the way to the beltway.

Carla rides up a path along the crest, sprawling brambles making it even narrower. Two excited puppies run down from above, a Labrador and a German shepherd, off-leash and wearing studded collars. They bark in greeting and run alongside her to the wrought iron gate.

The sign from a famous coffee shop in Amsterdam, the Bulldog, hangs at the entrance to the farm. Basma made the copy, identical to the original, with a PRUSA PRO 7, in memory of their first holiday together to celebrate managing to get a Permit of Stay two years ago. The only difference is that instead of the B there is a P and an S at the end, making it say PULLDOGS. The name of their community is a play on words, because they approach life like pull dogs.

There is an area on the left where a number of rickshaws are lined up, similar to those found in Monte Pincio park; they are the best means of transport for taking kids to the seaside in Focene. Behind the parking area, along the slope of the hill, is the kitchen garden where a few solar tarpaulins have been stretched between posts to form an automated greenhouse about thirty meters long. Inside this are about twenty planters for growing seasonal vegetables and last but not least, there is a well that provides water for the whole community.

At this time of day, it is Anna's turn to tend the garden. The Ukranian girl is wearing a GOGOL BORDELLO t-shirt and headphones, watering the plants and nodding her head like a woodpecker in time to the music. By the main building a pile of rough bricks produced by the shared printers is ready to be assembled into a pizza oven.

"I'm sorry, my love . . . but I never believed in the loan solution," Basma says from above, exhaling a trickle of smoke from an electronic cigarette loaded with a cannabis mixture. She is leaning against the stair bannister to catch the trickle of a breeze and enjoy the sight of her girlfriend, hot, sweaty and a little grumpy. She likes it when Carla pulls out her claws (or middle fingers), because then she needs comforting and they get to enjoy an unscheduled snuggle.

"I know, but we don't know enough people to crowdfund the amount we need."

As Carla comes up the stairs, Basma waves a letter at her that she had been hiding in her "claw," the three fingers she was left with after the accident with the mine.

"For you. It came this morning."

Carla leans into Basma's embrace, rests her head on her shoulder and takes the letter. The sense of momentary relief and safety lasts just until she has read the address of the sender of the registered letter.

"Oh fuck," she says, pulling away from Basma as if to isolate her from her irritation. "It's a Sant'Antioco postmark. Podda Legal Studio."

"We'd better sit down."

They go in and sit on the bench in the kitchen. The shared space can hold up to about twenty people, something that occasionally happens for a party or a birthday because the kitchen is normally in use at all times of the day, frequently during the night too; the heat of the season has imposed new rhythms, and every meal has been pushed back by six or seven hours: breakfast has moved to lunchtime, lunch to supper, and supper has become a middle of the night event.

Carla opens the envelope knowing it must concern her grandma Giuliana who died eight months ago.

She remembers the funeral she went to alone, without Basma. It was celebrated twice: the first, official ceremony took place in the Basilica di Sant'Antioco Martire and was attended by the mayor and a few other functionaries more interested in making themselves look good and promoting the attractive location than in mourning Giuliana Pinna. The second, informal moment had included everyone, apprentices, customers, friends, experts and enthusiasts, who had come to the laboratory of the maestro over the course of almost seventy years. Giuliana had lived for most of her life in the place that had been first a house and home, then a school, and finally a cultural center and even a city museum, spinning and weaving the extraordinary byssus fiber, sea silk, produced by the large mussel, the fan mussel, *pinna nobilis*.

"Finally, Grandma's will has got here," Carla says, reading it line by line. When she has finished reading, she can't hold back the tears. "She's left me her cloths."

"The sea silk ones?"

"Yes, but I feel bad, I didn't go to see her so often in her last years, we only kept in contact over Whatsapp. She was depressed too."

"Your grandmother? I can't believe it . . ."

"Yes, the town council opened the sea silk museum, but they argued almost immediately over the entrance fee. My grandmother wanted the museum to be free to everyone because sea silk weaving isn't a craft to sell. She believed in open source and open access before the terms were even invented. She wanted the museum to be a kind of free school."

"How did it end?"

Carla leans across the table to get the bottle of wine at the other end, half-fills a glass and downs it in one go.

"In the end the council closed the museum and turned the building into an old people's center with a pétanque pitch."

"No wonder she became depressed."

Carla pours another glass of wine and offers it to Basma, who copies her mode of drinking.

"But then . . ." Carla goes on, "my grandmother reopened the museum in her workshop and found an apprentice, finally someone worthy of the term, as she put it—who pulled her spirits up to no end."

Carla looks worried and Basma hugs her tight. "Good spirits that are not hereditary."

"What d'ya mean? Are you blind?" She says, laughing as an obstinate tear refuses to be stopped.

"So does this mean you have to go to Sant'Antioco?"

"Yes, I really don't think my mother has any desire to do it." She wipes her face and pushes the letter into her pocket.

"What about her share of the inheritance?"

She shrugs. "I don't know, the lawyer, Podda, will deal with it."

Carla's mother, Maria, had argued with Giuliana years before, and since then their relationship had become cold. Despite this, Carla, after moving to Rome, had kept in contact with her grandmother without her mother knowing about it. After all, their disagreements had nothing to do with her, though she was the object of their dispute: an old dispute that hadn't stopped causing grief to three generations of women in the Pinna family.

"Alright then, I'll look for my bathing suit and you book the dragon," says Basma with a wink. She always knew how to downplay a situation; she called the ship "dragonette" because she was convinced it would transport them to an enchanted place, like Sardinia. For someone like her, a survivor of the devastation in Syria, the comparison was valid.

The Pupil

The door to the workshop is closed and Carla doesn't even attempt to turn the handle. The sign with the maestro's opening times is still hanging on the door. It says:

WHEN I'M IN, IT'S BECAUSE I'VE ARRIVED

WHEN I'M NOT IN, IT'S BECAUSE I'VE GONE

IF YOU HAVEN'T FOUND ME, COME BACK LATER.

"What should we do?" Basma asks, worried.

"C'mon, when Grandma forgot her keys we went through here."

After a few steps down, Carla turns left into Vicolo Regina Margherita. She walks up the alley and stops by a little door in the back of the building.

"Wait for it . . ."

Carla counts the bricks from the bottom up, then left, up a bit more, slides a brick out from the wall and then turns it to reveal a hollow with a key taped in it. She puts the key in the lock, opens the door and leads Basma into the home-shop-workshop-museum of her grandmother Giuliana.

A stale smell is the first to hit their nostrils, then comes the salty odor of the sea, impregnated in the skeins of wool and linen scattered around the place.

Carla breathes in deeply. "I spent so many summers here. My grandmother used to say that a person could put on as many chic clothes as they wanted, but they would never be able to hide where they came from, in the same way that fibers can be dyed in many ways without ever removing their origins, or above all, their essence. Sea silk will never be linen or cotton…"

The house is composed of a large room divided into two sections: the back, where they came in, is the workshop, whereas the front portion topped by a stone vault, is where Giuliana, by her loom, welcomed the public. To the right is a kitchenette, the bedroom and bathroom are on the right. Basma leans on the bannister. "Where do the stairs go?"

"There's another room up there. When we came to Grandma's, Mom and I would sleep up there."

They can just about see various utensils hanging on the walls in the shadows, there are others scattered over the tables: old spools and shuttles, well-used distaffs, various sizes of spindles and carders, looms waiting to be mended. Here and there they can also see Giuliana's cloths and embroidery, passed down from generation to generation, starting from who knows when in the Pinna family's past, perhaps even with the notorious Princess Chaldea who came to Sardinia in ancient Roman times: fantastical animals defending women, birds like peacocks protecting the peace, images like stars and moons to guide vessels at sea, earthly and aquatic geometries, trees of life laden with fruit and ancient Nuragic towers. Behind every image there is a symbolic meaning, myths and legends, that had made Giuliana Pinna the last maestro of sea silk.

Strand after strand, all these fantastical universes had come to life on an ancient loom that was still there, all in one piece, which was currently strung with a linen warp and byssus weft. Her grandmother had used it right until the end with an agility that made it appear an extension of her own fingers. Now those memories start floating back up to the top of Carla's mind, fluctuating towards the past—bitter and sweet at the same time—leaving her drifting through so many experiences she had lived with her grandmother.

A shaft of light filters through the dark window, illuminating a piece of fabric

draped over a chair, amidst leaves, roots and bark. Its colors are vivid, going from bronze to ocher. Carla goes over and gently pulls it out from under a frame. Then, in shock, she realizes it isn't a frame, but fingers, thin and smooth. Lifting her eyes she can make out the lines of a face. She jumps back, hugging the cloth to her breast.

Curious, Basma looks closer and sees what appears to be an android, shut down and dusty.

"Oh, that thing nearly gave me a heart attack!" says Carla as soon as she recovers from the shock. "What's a thing like that doing here? It looks like a bank security guard in his cabin."

"Look, someone has written a message on its shoulders."

To Carla

This is Stephan, my assistant

He comes from Basel and knows how to weave the sea

He is part of your inheritance

We are in his hands

"Weave the sea," Carla repeats, almost lost in thought.

"Does that remind you of something?"

She sits at the loom, looks at the fabric and, as if hypnotized, begins to move her lips. A murmur comes from her mouth, a poetic chant:

Westerly, easterly, northwesterly, northeasterly
take my soul and throw it into the depths,

my life is for being, praying and weaving
for every person who comes to me and goes from me,
without land, without name, without borders, without
colors, without money,
for them I will bring the thread of the waters to the surface
for them I will weave the thread of the waters and it will
belong to all,
my prayer at dawn will belong to the woman and child
my prayer in the evening will belong to the man who accompanies them,
from them I will receive as much humility and peace as I
need to live healthily,
in the name of the Lion of my soul, the great Father and the
great Mother,
that is how it was, how it is, how it will be.
I swear.

"Oh, you're giving me goosebumps Carla, it sounds like a magic spell."

"It is, it's called the water oath. When the summer came, my grandmother would take me to the sea and get me to repeat it every other day and the days in between. There's a bay near here, a wonderful bay where fan mussels grow, they produce a kind of beard they use to defend themselves from octopuses and to anchor themselves to the seabed. My grandmother used to dive to four or five meters down and gather the filaments, which she turned into byssus, sea silk."

"I would like to see them."

"I'll take you tomorrow. First, we have to work out how to boot up Stephan."

Basma walks around the android and tries to inspect the body.

"It won't be easy, he's not just been shut down, I think he's also broken," she says, lifting Stefan's t-shirt to show the severed torso resting on the pelvis. The body has been cut into two parts: wires and cables dangle and hang limply from both.

Stephan begins to lean, and if Carla didn't run to hold him up he would have crashed straight to the ground.

At first the girls look at each other in shock, and then burst out laughing.

"I reckon Stephan did something very wrong."

"Do you reckon he made your grandma angry?"

SA GIUNCHERA

Leaving their bikes against a wall, Carla and Basma can resist no longer: drawn to the water, they pick up the pace and end up running down the beach, pulling their clothes off as they go, and jump into the refreshing, clear water.

Carla looks around, happy to see the place again. The last time, many years ago, her small hand had been in that of Giuliana, now she is holding Basma's under the water.

"When I was small and the *sirocco* came, my grandma would make me wear a tunic and an obsidian belt, then we were ready to dive. She would say we were going to collect mermaid hair as long as mine."

"So, this fantastic hair is down here, is it?"

"Exactly, extracting silk from the shells was fun, whereas having to desalt it for twenty-five days and change the water every day was deathly boring."

"Magic potions aren't easy to prepare, otherwise everybody would do it," says Basma, splashing at Carla.

"We also had to gather fifteen kinds of algae and put them together in a basin with lemon juice and sea water. The magic happened because the procedure took place during the lunar eclipse that happens every four years."

"So, no magic today?"

"No, today we are just exploring Sa Giunchera. You know how to dive, right? You'll see, it's spectacular down there!"

"I'm not an expert, but I'll survive!"

"Right then, take this," Carla says, handing her a thin rope. "If you get into difficulties give it a yank."

Basma makes the "ok" sign with her hand, with her claw it looks more like a rude gesture. Carla gives her a kiss and pushes her underwater, then guides her slowly downwards.

The joy of an underwater walk lasts as long as it takes to catch a glimpse of the seabed. Up until a few years ago this area was covered by endless meadows of seagrass, now it is a sandy desert covered by a mass of dead vegetation with dried-up stems sticking up here and there. Where, up until a few years ago, the oblong silhouettes of large mussels up to a meter and a half tall, like silent sentinels of the Sa Giunchera bay, could be seen, there are now only sixty odd empty shells, open and naked, leaning to one side or lying on the seabed—without even any octopuses taking refuge in the shells.

Carla fluctuates in this underwater cemetery as if she herself is a ghost, remembering the many times she and her grandmother had to chase the octopuses from the fan mussel fields. As soon as the octopuses found a partially open bivalve, basking in the sun filtering down from above, they would slide their tentacles in, eat the mussel and then take possession of the shell to use for their own home.

The spectacle they find before them now is even more horrible.

The cord becomes taut, and Carla looks around for Basma without seeing her. Then her eyes find her heading to the surface, the cord becoming even tighter. A few seconds later and they are back on the surface.

"Oh, I can't hold my breath for as long as you can," says Basma, drawing in a deep breath. "I would have fainted if we'd stayed down there any longer!"

"I'm sorry, but it's a disaster down there, it's a massacre. The last time I was here . . ."

"I bet it was very different."

"Yes, I am in shock! Fan mussels belong here in Sant'Antioco . . . and they should always be here. It makesno sense."

The devastation she has just seen reminds Basma of the land in Syria, she knows what it means to lose hope and the illusion that certain dramas don't actually happen to us. She had left two fingers to that tragedy thanks to a shrapnel mine on the road to school, but she managed to escape from the hellish place as soon as she could, whereas the fan mussels hadn't been able to and had lost their lives as they lost their homes.

Basma puts her arms around her girlfriend in this moment of mourning that seemed to be infinite: first Giuliana, and now the entire Sa Giunchera bay and its underwater inhabitants.

Suddenly, vibrations are running through them, the sea rises and Carla and Basma find themselves being jostled by waves moving them two or three meters. Basma looks out to sea and makes out the imposing silhouette of a cruise ship on its way to Carloforte.

"I reckon that monster wasn't here last time you were."

"I've lost my desire to swim."

"C'mon, let's go home. Poor old Stephan will be waiting for us."

ACCESS THE PAST, IGNITE THE FUTURE.

Carla had to buy three suitcases to put all the fabrics in. She also had to get a Fab Lab in Cagliari to print two large shaped packaging units to put Stephan in: one for his head, torso and arms, and one for his lower torso and legs. It was lucky he wasn't human and weighed less than twenty kilos.

In Sant'Antioco nobody would know how to put him back together and it was costing less to send him by courier than to buy him a berth on the ship, (always assuming they would have accepted him as a "pet," given his size). In the Serra Spina commune on the other hand, amongst the engineers, geeks and nerds they knew, the prospect of booting him back up was a lot more hopeful.

As they land in the harbor in Civitavecchia, Dikram waves to them from the dock, waiting with his rickshaw.

"Thanks for the lift, D! It feels like getting into a limo every time."

Dikram's vehicle has been modified to look like a ceremonial elephant: an illuminated trunk, a trumpeting horn, and flowing drapes woven with solar beads. The hydroponic flowerpots behind the bench provide his customers with fresh seasonal produce during their trip. When he rides down the street, everybody turns to look at this DIY wonder.

"For you, first class service always. Oh, and the courier came this morning. I've already unpacked Stephan at the FabLab and I've made a few calls. Valeria is going to help us; she's studying some tutorials."

"Ah, I can't wait to see what he has to tell us," says Basma enthusiastically. Carla on the other hand is more thoughtful about what Stephan might be able to reveal. After all, he did live with Giuliana for many years, certainly more than she had.

"Well, he won't ever be as good as new," says Dikram, "but with a bit of *jugaad* creativity we'll get him going again."

Once their baggage is in the luggage rack, Dikram and Basma begin to pedal on the tandem in the front while

Carla settles into the seat at the back. It takes them about two hours to get from the harbor in Civitavecchia to Serra Spino.

"Did you manage to sort things out with the legal studio? Certain cases can be brutal beasts," says Dikram.

"Yes, my mother has to deal with the last papers. The Sant'Antioco house will go to her."

"About that," says Basma, "can I ask you why she and Giuliana fell out? Did it have anything to do with the sea silk?

"Yes, it was about me too though."

"Do you want to talk about it?"

Carla watches the panorama of the Santa Marinella sea and the small houses lining the sides of Via Aurelia racing by beside her; on this side of the Tyrrhenian Sea, at a good emotional distance from Sant'Antioco, it is less painful to remember the arguments that ended up ruining her summers in Sardinia.

"Spinning and weaving was a noble art for Grandma, worthy of princesses and queens, like Penelope, Circe and Elena, all busy weaving wool, linen or sea silk. My mother didn't see it like that, weaving was an activity women were relegated to by men, the loom was their patriarchal cage. They were introduced to weaving when they were small, and then spent the rest of their lives at it as if in prison, dying, crucified by it, when they were old."

"That's a bit of a strong image."

Carla leans forwards towards the tulip turbines to feel a little wind.

"They were often very hard on each other. They were both feminists, on different sides. For my grandma sea silk was a sacred thing, a socio-cultural tool, a thread capable of binding the soul to water, a people to its land. She would have liked to have used this art for weaving "relationships," opening schools and academies. She dreamed of founding an international weaving school. My mother could never stand sea silk, perhaps because she felt squashed by my grandmother's personality and to affirm herself, she had to leave home at eighteen. She studied engineering in Rome, partly to show Giuliana that weaving was fit for an old fashioned world, not for the present day made up of electronics, coding and equal opportunities."

"Maybe they were both right."

"They were always arguing. For my grandmother, education and knowledge didn't count as much as experience alongside a maestro who knew how to transmit wisdom and hand on know-how. 'If you don't spend time with a maestro, you'll never become a maestro' she always said to people who visited her. For my mother, this approach wasn't scientific because it was based on an oral tradition, and therefore prone to interpretation and individual subjectivity, too close to magic and superstition for her liking."

After a number of kilometers, Dikram pulls over into a rest stop along Via Aurelia. Carla gets down, dries off the sweat and swaps places with Basma who takes the back seat.

"I imagine you were caught between the two fires."

All three drink from the elephant's tail in which a little tube connected to a reservoir in the frame of the rickshaw is hidden.

"Exactly," says Carla, handing the tail to Dikram. "My grandmother would have liked me to become a maestro to carry on the family tradition, but my mother couldn't wait for the summer to end so she could take me back to Rome. When I enrolled in the school of design and 3D modeling, she threw a party."

"It's a pity they couldn't get along."

A plane flies overhead, following the line of Via Aurelia towards Fiumicino.

"It was continual bickering," Carla yells to make herself heard. "As my grandma would have said, the fan shells of Sa Giunchera were murdered by bacteria brought on the keels of the Big Ships, as if many horses of Troy had come to bring us riches but at the same time contaminate our unpolluted lands, whereas my mother would say the problem was trawler fishing, acoustic pollution caused by yacht engines, eutrophication of the water caused by industrial waste dumping and global warming."

Once the rumbling of the plane has passed, loud trumpeting announces their return to the road.

In the past, before the arrival of the Pulldogs, the ground floor of Serra Spino had been a stall for cows and sheep. Now, though, in remembrance of its former agricultural use, the walls were hung with various farming implements, shovels, forks, scythes, and sickles. Dozens of purely decorative bales of hay disguise a server farm composed of batteries of racks full of flashing data-crunching cards. Each rack is mounted on wheels so that, if and when it is necessary, everything can be moved. The tendrils of the Pulldogs' rhizome extend from Pisa to Oslo, and from Chongqing to Lima: in their itinerant data center they develop mass-distributed computing projects and other open-source amenities. It all started with a contract from the Lazian regional administration assigning micro-seeding from incubators and business angels, but the money soon finished, and since then surviving had become a seasonal dance of sinking, rising and floating, the latest episode of which had a rather unhappy outcome at the San Paolo/Ostiense bank.

Some developers, with interactive gloves and augmented reality glasses, are busy programming from their padded chairs. They look like pilots in their cockpits facing wrap-around screens, ergonomic keyboards and holographic interfaces, the more prosaic reality is they are *peered,* seeking out hidden treasures in the crevices of the dark web and any NFTs idiotic enough to want to hack for the benefit of a needy community like themselves.

At the back of the stable, on a crate like a cat at the vet, is Stephan.

His legs swing to and fro as Valeria tests his knee reflexes. The torso has been inserted into the pelvic support and, despite the ugly welding scar circumnavigating his waist, is being held up by two planks of wood wedged under his armpits.

"Come, come here," she says, welcoming the group in. "We are making progress. This young man is sleeping, but his body works."

"So he booted up? Can he hear us?" Carla asks.

"He can, in theory. What do you say, Gennaro?" Valeria asks a big man smiling under his big thick beard, on a video call from Pisa.

"I'm just finishing a couple of things on the virtual machine, then we can ring his internal alarm clock," he replies, continuing to input data. "In the meantime, I can tell you Stephan was born in the TINPLAY laboratory in Turin, licensed by DAONICS. He was employed for three years at the Natural History Museum of Basel, in the section dedicated to fan mussels and sea silk. It's all in his memory log."

"How did he end up with my grandmother?"

"That information isn't in there, but since April 2019 he has never left Sardinia."

Stephan's eyelids open, and a sequence of ocular movements together with acoustic signals indicate his coming online. Everybody is waiting for him to say something, or introduce himself, instead his fingers start to move: small movements, precise movements made up of twisting and pinching, gentle pushes and lateral movements. These gestures become more pronounced and begin to include his wrists, the movements become more complex, a coordinated articulation of agile pinching and punctual releases, sudden folding and repeated pulling, as if Stephan were "picking up the threads" of something unfinished when he was shut down.

Basma's own hands fly to her mouth. "Have you seen his nails?"

"I hadn't noticed," Carla answers as she moves towards the moving hands: she recognizes these movements, repeated thousands of times by Giuliana. The long, smooth nails don't look like they belong on Stephan, or at least four of them are clearly fake, attached to the nail bed with glue, while the others must have fallen off showing their original shape.

A part of Carla wants to put her arms around that stranger, another would rather keep her distance. "Stephan, can you hear me?" she asks, embarrassed but curious.

The android turns, hands still weaving as if this has priority over everything else.

"Why were you shut down? How did you end up broken?"

Stephan looks from left to right, realises he is no longer in the Sant'Antioco workshop, and speaks, "Where is the maestro? The maestro has all the answers."

The people present look at each other perplexed.

"The maestro isn't here," Carla tries to reassure him. "Can *you* give us the answers?"

"Yes, I can answer for the maestro, but I didn't mean to do it. It was an error. Too hot."

"What error are you talking about?"

"The accident."

That day a few months ago when Carla's mother had called her to tell her Giuliana had fallen and been taken to hospital. Only a few days later she was dead from complications following a concussion.

"My mother never said how it happened, only that Giuliana fell while she was working."

"Indeed, this is the reason why I was shut down." Stephan pauses, and his hands stop. They start moving as he starts talking again, "As you said 'my mother,' you must be Carla, the maestro's heir."

She is embarrassed by hearing that definition said in a way that appears to refer, rather than to the legal inheritance from Giuliana, to the spiritual one.

"Yes, we meet finally. I know nothing about you, I haven't been to Sant'Antioco for years."

"I, on the other hand, know you well from Giuliana's stories."

He makes a move to stand up. He jumps down from the table and the wooden planks fall to the floor. He goes to Carla and hugs her—clumsily but with warmth—as though she were a relative. She blushes and reciprocates the gesture cautiously, looking impotently at Basma, eyes to the sky in surprise.

Carla tries to bring the conversation back to the mystery of Stephan. "Now, can you tell me why you were shut down?"

"The day after Giuliana was taken to the hospital, Maria ran to the hospital of Sant'Antioco and then came to the workshop. She was very sad, as if I had disappointed her. She asked me to reproduce the scene of the accident because Giuliana told her it was I who made her trip after being admonished, and she didn't believe it."

Stephan accesses the memo. His eyes project a swathe of light showing the workshop from his point of view. In the background they can hear a guttural singing, a repetition of a sequence of strange phonemes: Oinnamaaa . . . oimmamaiaa . . . oinnamaaa . . . oinnammaia . . . oinnamaaa . . . oimmamaiaa . . .

"I was trying to copy her voice, the tone of her singing, the rhythm of the litany, but she got angry every time."

"It doesn't work without a soul!" Giuliana's shouting bursts into the virtual room. She waves her knitting needle in the air as if she were an orchestra conductor. "We have been trying for months and months. I will tell Maria, next time I see her, that you are no good! You are not suitable to take over from me!"

"Maestro, there is no hurry. The more time we spend together the more in tune we become."

"In tune?! We're not on the radio! Weaving requires agility, competence, patience and high precision of style, all things you possess an abundance of, more than any other apprentice or maestro I have ever met . . . But you don't have any passion."

Stephan's hands stop moving in mid-air.

"C'mon, get up! We're going to Sa Giunchera, if you can survive some free diving perhaps the soul of this place will grow within you."

"I got up from the loom," Stephan takes up the tale again, straightening his back at the memory of those words. "It was the first time the maestro had ever asked me to go to the sea with her. I was so happy and excited."

Stephan's sudden outburst takes Giuliana by surprise and she takes a step backwards instinctively. In his hurry to obey Stephan knocks into her unintentionally; she loses her balance, trips and hits her head as she falls. In the simulation they see Stephan reaching out to her in an attempt to stop her from falling, but she slips through his fingers.

As the simulation stops, the atmosphere is tense. Everyone has lowered their heads, and Carla squeezes her eyes shut, her hands becoming fists.

"I've never been to Sa Giunchera," he adds with an almost inhuman candor.

"Then what happened?"

"I tried to help her, she didn't respond. I called emergency services, the ambulance reached us fifteen minutes later. The following day I tried to explain to Maria that it had been an accident." Stephan continues, "But she wouldn't listen to me, she said nobody would ever believe the word of an android."

"That makes no sense, this video confirms that you didn't do it on purpose."

"That is the reason she ordered me to shut down."

"Couldn't she have just deleted the file from your memory?"

"My memory isn't only local, there is a version on the cloud."

"So it would have been useless," Carla sinks into a tangle of thoughts that make her uncomfortable. "Perhaps my mother was afraid everyone would see her failure. After ordering you to shut down, she could have been the one to damage you. More out of anger than anything else . . ."

"I cannot know this. Perhaps you can tell me?" Stephan asks, looking at the people present. They all look at him dumbfounded.

Carla can imagine her mother, in a moment of anger, destroying Stephan almost as a way of punishing herself: she was the one who had wanted Stephan to take her place by Giuliana's side; it had been her idea to propose this as the solution to perpetuate a tradition that would otherwise come to an end. If the passing down from woman to woman wasn't going to work, maybe that from woman to android could fill the gap until a future heir could be found.

Carla promises herself that she will talk to Maria about this, but in the meantime, she wants to explore another aspect of this sequence of events. She pulls a handkerchief from her pocket, embroidered with a reddish face, and offers it to Stephan. "Do you know her?"

"Of course, that is Berenice of Cilicia, princess of Chaldea and daughter of King Herod Agrippa, who fell in love with Titus, son of the emperor Vespasian Augustus and future king of Rome. Judeo-Christian tradition sees her as a sinner, but perhaps the tragic story of her love was made so impossible by palace conspiracies, forcing her into an exile that led her to Sant'Antioco. Here the princess started the sea silk tradition and taught the women to gather and weave the precious fiber. To be precise, this is a portrait of Berenice in keratinized collagen, sea silk, using a stitch known as *punto di pensiero* and bleached in a solution of *Posidonia*, *Padina pavonica* and *Caulerpa*, steeped in seawater, lemon juice and citron. The red coloration is achieved by dyeing the fiber with saffron flowers and salt, we used the residue of this, diluted in ten liters of water, as fertilizer for the kitchen garden behind the workshop. I made that handkerchief myself four years ago. One of my first pieces to earn approval from the maestro."

"What else do you know how to do?" Carla asks, looking at Basma with a pinch of mischievousness.

"Like the maestro, I know 189 types of stitching. I can teach tailoring, weaving, crochet, knitting . . . I have over 654

"Have you ever used a 3D printer?"

"No, but I learn fast."

Basma winks at Carla.

WEFT

"Why didn't you tell me about Stephan?" Carla asks her mother over the video call.

"You wouldn't have understood."

Maria is working in the TINPLAY workshop in Turin surrounded by mechanical limbs and android prototypes, some even more advanced than Stephan. Behind her, dogs patter, ballerinas twirl and a six-armed pizza chef spins six pizzas.

"What would I not have understood? That Grandma wanted me to become a maestro, but you had other plans?"

"Plans you have never even considered."

"This again! I never wanted to become an engineer."

"At least by now you would have had a decent job and house."

"Here we go again. I am fine at Serra Spino, I like digital craftsmanship. Is that a sin? Can you really not just accept me as I am?"

"I have always tried to respect your choices, but that doesn't mean I have to be happy about watching you waste your life."

Carla says nothing. The same old dead-end conversation leading to nowhere except a deep valley of profound resentment. There is the same distance between Carla and her mother as there was between Maria and Giuliana. She doesn't feel as if she is between two fires—like Basma said— but a long way away from both.

"Well, y'know what I say? I've put Stephan back together. He is here with me and says hello."

She turns her cell phone to show Maria Stephan raising his hand to wave. With the other hand, to which a nozzle connected to five reservoirs of material has been attached, he is printing an object.

"Why did you do that? He's dangerous. He made Giuliana fall . . ."

"Stop it, he is not dangerous. I saw the recording of the accident."

It is Maria's turn to stay silent. Behind Carla Stephan's oblong creation is taking shape, layer after layer: a flower petal.

"I don't have the proof, but I think it was you who broke him."

"I suppose Stephan told you this?"

"No, he couldn't, but he did tell me about the Maker Fair in Germany, about the digital crafts project and your proposal to TINPLAY to send him to Grandma to develop his weaving techniques."

"It was a mistake. She never wanted him."

"You see? It hurts when someone won't accept what you want."

"So, what are you proposing to do with him?"

Carla turns the cell phone around again. The petal is complete, and Stephan is looking at it with a bright intensity in his eyes. Then he inserts it into a slot in the corolla of a blue flower: he has just created a replacement petal for damaged wind tulips.

"I don't know, for the moment he is helping here in the FabLab. Please thank TINPLAY for us."

Stephan blows on the tulip whirligig, whose petals begin to rotate around the center.

It's late in the night when Basma lies down in bed next to Carla.

The room is full of wearable technology: t-shirts with weather-changing fibers, shoes with extendable heels, water-repellent jackets, and various other projects Carla and Basma have been working on for months. It was these inventions—a mixture of traditional craftsmanship and native innovation—that brought them together four years previously at the Rome edition of the Maker Fair.

"Can't you sleep?"

"No, I can't stop thinking about the fan mussel cemetery in Sa Giunchera"

"About that, we haven't been to your grandmother's grave in Sant'Antioco yet."

"You're right. My mother wanted to cremate her because there was no room left in the family tomb. She was buried in an ossuary in the municipal cemetery. That's no place for her."

The rustle of the tulips on the windowsill is relaxing. A breath of breeze is enough to produce sufficient energy for the workshop, even at night.

"Exactly, it would be better if she could stay in Sa Giunchera with her fan mussels," Basma says, taking Carla's face between her hands. "That's where she should be laid to rest, don't you think?"

"It's a lovely idea, but how can we possibly get her out?"

Basma stops talking; she thinks hard, biting her lip and fiddling with a strand of her hair. The rustling from the window gets louder, the tulips are being driven by the west wind, the *ponentino*.

"Don't think about her ashes. I think I have an idea. Do you have a photo of the urn?"

"Of course, I chose it, my mother didn't feel up to it. So, do we have to go back to Sant'Antioco?"

"Yes, and this time Stephan will be able to walk on his own two feet."

"What's going through that mind of yours?"

"The other day I was telling Stephan about Sa Giunchera," says Basma, taking a tuft of sea silk from the nightstand. "He was so sad at not having been able to go to the bay. He wanted so badly to come close to the molluscs he has heard so much about. It almost felt like he wanted to pay homage to them for the gift of sea silk."

"Maybe you just projected your wishes onto him."

Basma holds the tuft of sea silk out to Carla; it is so light it feels weightless.

"Look, these fibers are different from the others because Giuliana—according to Stephan—discovered a way of taking the silk from the fan mussels without damaging the mollusc. She studied their habitat for years, she dived in every season, sun, rain or wind. With the experience she gained she realized that in May, the sea bed in the bay is softer and spongier and it's possible to pull out the molluscs, cut a portion of the rough, unkempt fibers and 'plant' it again without it dying. This way the keratinized collagen filaments can regrow, and the mollusc doesn't suffer."

"Did he tell you that?"

"Well, yes, while he was showing me his memo," says Basma.

"All right then," says Carla. She takes her cell phone, pulls up a site and shows Basma an image. "This is the urn, a simple wooden cube with an engraved plaque."

Basma takes a photograph of it and kisses her girlfriend. "We can book the *dragonette* tomorrow!"

It is three in the morning when Stephan's eyes light the footpath running behind the Sant'Antioco cemetery. After a few meters of scrub his headlights shine on a

three-meter-high wall.

"This is a good place, can you do it?" Basma asks as Carla looks around cautiously.

"Yes, I just have to calculate the force needed."

In the time it takes to count to three, Stephan bends his legs and jumps so high he grabs the top edge of the wall. He sits astride it and from there lowers a rope for the others.

Once they are in, they head quietly towards the Pinna family columbarium.

In front of Giuliana's burial recess, the lowest of six, Carla pulls a bunch of flowers from her backpack and puts them in the vase, replacing the dried-out ones. In the meantime, Basma lays out a selection of building tools in front of her, including a bucket and a bottle of water. With the help of Stephan's multi-purpose fingers, she gets ready to remove the slab sealing the burial recess.

"My brother works in the building sector," she says to Carla, worried about being found out and reported to the police, "and he has taught me a few tricks. In an hour we will be out with Giuliana under our arms."

Stephan pulls out his right index finger and offers Basma the empty socket, where she inserts a precision drill bit. The plaster on the slab comes away easily under three thousand micro-blows per minute, and after not long Stephan proffers his left-hand index finger to her. Carla hurries to clean it all up with a portable vacuum cleaner.

"Right then, now we can go in."

The chisel mounted on Stephan's left-hand digs into the plaster, creating flakes and dust. After five minutes the slab begins to move.

"Now slow it down," says Basma, "and angle the point at a thirty to forty degree incline."

Stephan does as she says and after another circuit of the perimeter, the slab comes away in Carla's hand, who was waiting ready to catch it.

"Now let's do our magic and pull out the maestro."

Basma takes an urn out of her backpack, it is identical to the one containing Giuliana's ashes, and swaps them: the same material, same plaque, but printed by the Fab Lab two days earlier.

"A pleasure to meet you, Giuliana," she says, half-serious, half-facetious. "I will leave you in your granddaughter's hands." She passes the urn to Carla and begins to prepare the plaster: she extracts some plaster mixed with clay from a bag and pours it into the bucket adding enough water to make a soft but not too liquid paste. In the meantime, Stephan has replaced his index fingers and is now holding a trowel in one hand and a float in the other.

"Take the cement with the back of the trowel," Basma tells him. "And throw it with a sharp snap at the area to be plastered. Whatever falls should be collected and re-mixed. Each layer must be smoothed and left to harden before going on to the next. Always from the bottom to the top. Understand?" He nods.

The speed with which Stephan works is amazing, as is his coordination and precision. At a certain point another beam of light cuts through the darkness of the cemetery, pointing towards them.

"Quick, turn everything off," Carla hisses as she hurries to hide behind the columbarium. Basma follows her, but Stephan remains where he is.

"Hey! Come away, you'll get yourself caught."

The mysterious light is intense and is coming from four or five meters above. When it reaches Stephan's face, the light begins to flash, sending sequences similar to Morse code. Even Stephan's eyes are flashing jerkily, a kind of stroboscope effect, but at the end of the exchange the drone leaves the same way it came.

"What just happened? What did you say?" Carla asks, coming out of a niche.

"That I am repairing the ruined plasterwork on a columbarium."

"In the middle of the night?" Basma says.

"Of course, so it will be as good as new tomorrow."

"Why wasn't it suspicious?" Carla insists.

"Androids carry on working even when humans sleep."

"You're amazing," say Carla and Basma in unison. The three hug each other as if they have just won the lottery.

"Can we go to the bay now?"

Basma goes back to smoothing the second layer of plasterwork.

"First we're going to get this job done, then we will take you to the sea."

Fun-Lab

Sa Giunchera is amazing with its rainbow of colors: the blue of the sky and sea frame the yellow ochre and brown splashes of the Mediterranean maquis dotted with the red berries of mastic shrubs and the green dots of juniper bushes.

A number of inaccessible cliffs create rocky alleys leading to the golden beach.

"Here, this is for you," Carla says, handing Stephan a diver's drysuit.

"But I am waterproof!"

"You may well be, but it's best not to run the risk."

He makes a noise like a resigned sigh and puts on the diving suit.

"So you must carry the ashes." Stephan takes the urn from his shoulder bag, and hands it to Carla. "You must do it; you are her heir."

She weighs the responsibility and in the end decides that she doesn't feel up to the task. "You spent more time with her, you were her assistant. I barely know the oath. You are the last maestro."

"Alright, even though your grandmother only considered me a device and you were always her choice."

Carla's steps become heavy: accepting this title from an android seemed so out of the ordinary; as far as it went, Giuliana had never considered herself a craftsman whose experiences and knowledge had to be preserved in the name of tradition; there had always been much more at stake than her weaving business. Her grandmother's business wasn't selling, she taught. A maestro doesn't earn a living selling drapes and fabric, a maestro creates art that should be considered an asset for all, for the development and balance of humanity.

When she was small, Carla imagined Giuliana was a kind of witch-pirate, and just like those legendary figures, clothed in magic and strange powers, she knew how to create amazing stories, fantasy tales and grand ideals like amulets and objects of defence against evil, because when it came down to it, her grandmother had simply attempted to defend herself and her way of life from the attacks and threats of the local powers who wanted to turn Sant'Antioco into a tourist harbor for the mooring of Big Ships and the subsequent landing of the barbarians.

Seeing her doubt, Basma goes to her. "Are you all right? Ready to weave the sea?"

"I remember a summer's day," Carla says, lost in thought. "I had been misbehaving, I was being impossible, nothing would please me. I didn't want to eat, go out or sleep. My grandmother came to me holding a spindle with thread in her hands..."

All three go into the sea, the water comes up to their knees.

"'Weaving is a way of being,' she said in that dramatic way of hers, 'that teaches patience and restores confidence: the warp is already in our lives, like it is on the looms, but depending on the weft each of us weaves in, our differing futures and the carpet on which the new generations will walk are created.'"

Step by step, they go in up to their hips.

"At the time I didn't understand the meaning of her words, but now I think my grandmother's stories and gestures stuck to me like threads of sea silk, of fan mussels, she wove a tapestry inside me that would be impossible to undo."

Stephan places a hand on the lid of the urn. "I'm ready."

"Me too," says Carla.

Lifting the lid, Stephan scatters the ashes over the water around them.

"In the end, the maestro has gone back to her beloved fan mussels," he says.

Basma and Carla exchange a worried look. He doesn't know what has happened down there yet.

"Stephan, we have to show you something."

They take him by the hand and lead him further out to sea, to the area where Giuliana always used to dive. He is making odd little sounds, as if he is anxious. He is about to explore the world he has wanted to know for years.

Below the surface of the sea his underwater vision is clear, his hearing captures muffled sounds and he can identify a number of colorful fish swimming around him; below him, though, he can barely see the sand, covered as it is by a carpet of compacted, dead seagrass. Then he makes them out: the oblong outlines of the fan mussels lying on the seabed, like shipwrecks. All dead. There are no threads of sea silk, nor bivalves doing their filtering, and no sign of the molluscs he had come to know through Giuliana's stories.

He stays down there for a long time, until Carla decides to dive again to bring him to the surface. She finds him on the seabed stroking an old, encrusted shell.

When he surfaces Stephan makes a sad sound, melancholy, regretful.

"I got here too late. The fan mussels have gone . . ."

"We wanted you to see with your own eyes. Perhaps it was the Big Ships, perhaps it was the eutrophication of the water, whatever the cause, the result is tragic," says Carla.

"We have to hurry up then."

"Hurry up? For what?"

Stephan goes back to the shore. He has accelerated his movements. Carla and Basma look at each other nonplussed and hustle to follow him. Not long later they see him taking off the diving suit, pressing a place on his chest and opening a compartment in his thorax they hadn't noticed before. They see him pulling out a smock, the same one Giuliana used to use, which he had been looking after inside him, and putting it on. Lastly, they see him pull a ring out of the compartment and put it on a finger.

"Stephan, can I ask you what you're doing?"

"Of course, now that the maestro has gone, we have to find someone to take her place."

"But you are the closest thing to a maestro Giuliana has ever instructed."

"That's right, but nobody will see me as a maestro, just like nobody believes my word, like Maria said. Also, I do not have an apprentice, which is just as risky. It is always better if there is a maestro and an apprentice."

"Are you saying that should be me?"

"Yes, I could be the supply maestro, until you take my place."

Carla relies on Basma's intuition, and her hint of a smile is worth more than hundreds of words.

"Let's do it."

"From now on," Stephan says, solemnly repeating Giuliana's litany, "I leave and you arrive. Everything you have learned, you already have; everything you haven't learned, you will learn. Have a good life." Then he pulls off the smock and hands it to Carla, who takes it and puts it on.

"Aren't I supposed to be the apprentice?"

"Yes, but you are also the heir, so this is an exception. Do you remember the water oath?"

"Of course, Giuliana made me learn it by heart."

"Good, this is the moment."

While Carla repeats the words, Stephan slides off the ring and rests it on the sand. When she has finished saying the words of the oath, Carla picks up the ring and puts it on.

Basma moves closer to her quietly: "One day I would like to marry you this way."

There is a bit of a commotion in front of the museum-workshop. There are a number of people walking along Via Regina Margherita while others are already queuing. Stephan is carrying a tray of sandwiches in one hand and one of pastries in the other. Carla is on her phone, "Yes, I'm sure," she says, raising her eyes to the sky, "and please don't call me again, we're not interested, goodbye," and hangs up.

"Him again?" Basma asks from her position at the top of a ladder in front of the entrance.

"Yes, he said he's seen a lot about sea silk on various TV channels and print media: Rai 1, Rai 2, Canale 5, Italia 1, *Bell'Italia*, Meridiani, *Airone*, *Le Figaro*, *The New York Times*, *Die Welt*, *National Geographic*, CNN and the BBC . . . He has realized the potential of the project and wants to offer us financial help with a part of this being non-repayable or jointly funded."

"But sea silk mustn't be commercialized, it mustn't be bought and sold! It's a giiift!" Basma says in a sing-song voice, making fun of the consultant like Giuliana would have done. Then she turns to the others. "Is it straight?"

Stephan's eyes project a line around the sign showing exactly the desired position.

"Thank you, that's great."

SEA SILK MUSEUM
FUN-LAB

"There you go, you see? Everything is ready, even without financing."

Carla pushes the doors of the workshop wide open and invites the waiting people in. There are parents with their children, groups of teenagers, friends of Giuliana and other curious people from all over Sardinia.

"Welcome! Today we are inaugurating a very special place, a museum-workshop open to everyone with the aim of creating a supportive community to learn the wisdom of the past, enhance the value of the present day know-how and explore the possibilities of the future.

Inside, two of Basma's PRUSA PRO 7s have been placed close to Giuliana's loom and are churning out parts to assemble other printers. All the projects the women have uploaded to the cloud, from the plausible to the bizarre, will soon become reality: low cost medical prosthetics, self-cleaning sheets and weather-changing fibers, and that's just the start. Giuliana's workshop is destined to merge with Carla and Basma's digital crafts workshop.

Stephan might have less powerful and resistant arms than a KUKA model, but he is definitely more sensitive and suitable for their purposes.

He is surrounded by children, intent on telling them the

history and uses of the strange spinning and weaving tools most of them have never seen before.

"Look, it's sparkling!" A small child says in amazement.

"Is it precious?" Asks a small boy.

"Oh yes, it's more precious than you might think. 'Sea silk' is obtained from the fibers of the *Pinna nobilis*, a mollusc known as the fan mussel. It anchors itself to the sandy seabed," he says, showing them a specimen over a meter long. "In Sa Giunchera there was a colony, but now it has gone, exterminated by pollution. In the past, the clothes of kings, sovereigns and the world's most powerful people were made with sea silk. It was harvested and processed by the "water women," priestesses of the sea who lived on the shores of the Mediterranean. The weaving of it took place there, on a loom made from cane," Stephan says, pointing to the contraption. They follow the direction of his finger in amazement, "And you have to use your nails to slide the warp threads to make designs in the weft. The last maestro of sea silk was Giuliana Pinna, I was her apprentice while we waited for the arrival of her heir and the next maestro," he ends by turning towards Carla.

"Are you thinking of opening other places like this one? I come from Brindisi... and I heard there are fan mussels in our sea too," a tourist says to Stephan.

"I don't know, but if the sea is there. Perhaps they are not the same kind of fan mussels, but a similar kind of mussel. If there are no molluscs, you could use the threads from a banana tree, a caterpillar or a coconut. The important thing is to teach people to weave, not to move the loom; the thread is an excuse to come here, to meet up, to talk to each other and get to know each other, and in the meantime, they weave, and without realizing it, weave life."

Carla has tears in her eyes: those are the very same words her grandmother would have used, spoken in the same tone as she would have used. Maybe the dive at Sa Giunchera really had brought Stephan a soul, perhaps the magic of that place made no distinction between human or artificial beings, so long as it continued to exist.

Basma takes Carla to one side and whispers in her ear, "The tourist has a point, it's not too late."

"What do you mean?"

"I mean, if your grandmother learned to take the fan mussels from the seabed and then put them back unharmed, we could try to transplant them too."

"They would die. Sa Giunchera is doomed."

"Maybe not. We have Stephan now."

Carla pulls the cell phone from her beach bag and makes a call. Lying beside her, Basma is enjoying the spring sunshine; it is already thirty-five degrees and it is only April.

"Ciao Ma, how are you?"

"I'm fine, and you? How is the project going?"

"Great, the home-workshop is really useful. We are doing lots of activities."

"That's good. It would be a pity to have to sell it."

"Have you had any news about the proposal?"

"Not yet, but the TINPLAY board is meeting this week. I'm fairly confident."

Basma wakes up and asks Carla to put the call on speakerphone.

"Hello Maria, you are so generous to allow us use of the house. I hope you can come see us soon!"

"Hello Basma, yes, as soon as I can free up some time I'll get on a ferry and come visit you."

Basma is about to add something, but Carla stops her, holding up a finger as a sign to wait.

"Would you like to see him? He is here in front of us."

"Yes, of course, turn the phone around."

Carla points the phone's camera at the sea and attempts to focus on a distant point.

"I can't see anything."

"Wait a moment," says Carla, zooming in. Stephan's head looks like a yellow marker buoy. Actually, they have dyed his hair yellow to make him more visible in the middle of the sea.

"The leisure"

"Incredible! Is it working?"

"Oh yes, you should see how his eyes flash when a Big Ship comes close to the area where the fan mussel nursery is, sometimes he even imitates the sound of children shouting to scare the AI pilots," Carla says, amused.

"And if some show-off on a speedboat insists on causing trouble," Basma adds as her head appears in the frame, "he sounds the alarm sirens, eardrum-bursting frequencies that make anybody threatening the tranquillity of the molluscs keep their distance."

"Really clever, I will do everything I can to convince the board to send you another Stephan."

"Thank you, ah, just one more thing . . ." says Carla, turning the cell phone back around. She puts an arm around Basma's shoulders and pulls her in against her.

"In three months, we will be celebrating a year of the funlab and . . ." Basma encourages Carla to finish, "We're going to take advantage of the occasion to get married."

"Ah, what wonderful news! I am so happy for you. Now I have another reason to come back to Sardinia."

"Thank you, we can't wait to see you," they say together.

Once the call has finished, Carla and Basma jump in the water and dive down. When they reach the seabed, they explore the colony transplanted some months ago. Small filaments are beginning to guild the shells just beginning to open to catch the sunlight. Not far off, Stephan waves at them. He has just finished unrolling a skein of fibers on the seabed that are the protective net for the sea silk cultivation. Every week he verifies the state of decomposition of the net. It was printed in the Fab Lab from organic material and he replaces the most damaged portions. Then, from the compartment in his chest, he takes a handful of seagrass seed and replants them in the underwater meadow.

PROLOGUE

You look at the sky over the Porta di Roma shopping centre knowing your revenge will come soon.

The clouds of starlings thicken and stretch like cotton-wool clouds in spring, light grey, joyous, cinematographic and totally innocuous. Only today is Christmas day, and those starlings are twisting in the air like memories of the terrible experiences you have had in this place over the last few months. Snickers. Reports. Questioning. Isolation. Pushing and shoving. Humiliation.

Now you know that the enemy of your enemy may be your friend.

Now you know that plants and their rhizosphere may become a defence at the same time as being salvation for a decadent society.

SIX MONTHS EARLIER
THE GRUEN SYNDROME

Beep.

The security guard dozing in front of the screen showing CCTV images from the sixty-two cameras placed throughout Porta di Roma raises his eyes.

Beep. Beep.

He grimaces resignedly at the emotional recognition of CCTV #476

Beep. Beep. Beep.

He grabs his cell, clicks on the AGA app and leaves the control room.

His target is the angry and anxious expression that crosses your face as soon as you have spent over sixty minutes in a shopping center, though in Porta di Roma your resistance time is reduced to forty. This is why your moves are rapid and efficacious, no distractions, no deviating, straight to the final destination, assuming you can find it in time.

"Good morning, I'm sorry to disturb you. Are you feeling okay?"

The guard appears in front of you, blocking your way forward.

"Yes, why?"

"Your AGA index is very low."

You are still lucid and allow yourself a pinch of irony.

"Look, I don't like Lady Gaga. I only listen to Metal."

"You don't understand, AGA stands for Auto-Gratification from Acquisition."

You shrug, but an alarm is already sounding in your head. How many seconds are you wasting?

"So?"

"So, I want to know why you came here?"

You look at him nonplussed; he could be a classmate from secondary school. One of the ones who used to snicker behind the chemistry teacher's back. One of the ones who made fun of anyone, for the stupidest things. One of the ones who now, like many, has a meaningless job, where he is prompted by CCTV, led by an app and evaluated by an algorithm.

"Why? Does there have to be a special reason? I need a new pair of underwear. Do you want a sniff?"

You're spitting acid and at the same time you shield your eyes with your hand from the flashing lights coming from the shops EXTYN and JONNYJOY, the colored neon signs over at IDEXE and the flashing sequences from

OKAIDI. The fluorescence emanating from the PIMKIE shop window is too far away to bother you.

He doesn't give up, "No, of course not, but . . . don't you want to buy anything else?"

"Well," you say, pulling a crumpled flier from the pocket of your trousers. "There are the supermarket's special offers of the week."

"Special offers of the week," he repeats, mimicking you, a little scornfully. He shakes his head and grabs you by the arm, "have to test you, nothing personal, security measures."

Now you stick a finger in your right ear in an attempt to unblock it: the pop music blaring out from CLAYTON forces you to raise your voice. The auto-tune of the song coming from the SONNY BONO satellite speakers makes your skin crawl.

"Oh, there's no need to test me, I'm clean."

"It's not drugs," he protests. "Thirty seconds and we're done! You only have to look at some images and tell me what you see."

Thirty seconds added to what you have already lost will make you risk it big. "All right . . ." you say resignedly. It's the first time you have found yourself in this kind of situation because all the other times in here ended with:

- someone telling you off for bad manners
- someone pointing at you as you turn pale
- someone making fun of you because you lost your sense of direction
- someone fanning your face with a brochure
- someone slapping your face to wake you up
- someone bringing you something to drink after vomiting
- someone holding you after you passed out
- someone lifting you up and putting you back on your seat in the shuttle bus

-     someone giving you a lift to Tufello

He continues to the test, opens the app and shows you a series of animals in their natural habitats on his cell: a jaguar, a bunny, a camel, a crocodile and a pony.

"Do you recognize these?"

You don't see the animals like 97% of test subjects do, you don't see that they look like the stylized logos of product brands, you see what surrounds them, the trees, the bushes, the brambles, and none of these luxuriant or arid sceneries make you blind to green.

"Of course, forest, countryside, desert, swamp and a field."

Your AGA index crumbles and falls below the acceptable level: you are a commercial danger, a walking risk for people shopping in peace. The security guard's expression changes, he pockets his cell, takes you by the arm and this time drags you down the corridor. "You can't stay here. I have to escort you off the premises."

"Oh, leave me alone! What the hell are you doing?! I'm fine."

"I know," he says as the app sends warnings from his trouser pocket as if you are full of shrapnel bombs, "this is for the welfare of our customers."

"But I'm agoraphobic! I'll buy my pantiesand leave. I swear!"

"I'm sorry. The negative experience of one customer must not influence that of others."

You try to resist. You try to dig your heels in. He yanks you along. You scrabble to find any kind of handhold. Everything is so smooth and clean in here it slips past beneath your hands without giving you anything to grab on to. Then, almost as if it had been you to attack him, the security guard pulls out his pepper spray.

"No, no, all right, I'll stop."

So you go limp and let him drag your dead weight along. You become a dull, oblong strip sliding along the shiny-as-a-mirror pavement. Passers-by look at you with the usual expressions of indifference/scorn/disbelief, only slightly different to those you frequently see on their taut faces as they hunt for discounts and unmissable special offers.

The security guard leaves you in the central forecourt of Porta di Roma. He dumps you there as if you were a cumbersome sack of rubbish beneath the towering walled-in *Ailanthus Altissima*. The tree has also been shunned, it has also been denied entrance, it is considered a weed.

You fall to the ground, a ball of shame. "Bastards."

"Oh yeah, they really are a bunch of bastards," you turn, and before any image comes into focus a wave of intense smells you can't identify washes over you. "I saw how that particular bastard treated ya."

The man emanating the strange smells is a bizarre character: he has flowers and plants all over him: in the pockets of his ragged coat, under his baseball cap, in the cuffs of his frayed jeans, under the collar of his flowery shirt, poking through his belt. They are even woven into the beard hanging from his chin: long, grey and thick.

His clothes drip with flowers and are lined with leaves.

"That's never happened to me before," you say, perplexed, as you get up.

"It's the current policy of consumerism." He holds out a hand to pull you up.

"What do you mean?"

"It means they don't like people like us."

"What do you mean, *people like us*?"

"You an' me are different. Lemme show you something."

He pulls out his cell, opens an app and shows you the screen.

"Oh no, not another app! This time there are clouds. What are they supposed to be?"

Globular splodges bob across the screen, known as VOCs—they represent various concentrations of Volatile Organic Compounds. You read this on the app because otherwise for all you know they could also be another brand of women's underwear.

"You an' me have the same syndrome."

You take a couple of steps backwards and look at him sideways.

"Syndrome? I don't have any syndrome."

"Oh yeah, you do . . . It's called the Gruen syndrome, you see this stuff? It's emitted by all the products in the shopping center, despite the air purifiers, Dyson gadgets and whatnot. Ain't nothing can be done; they emit chemical compounds and in high concentrations they are toxic."

"But I'm not allergic, I've never had bad reactions to chemical products."

"Are you sure 'bout that? Tell me, 'ow long can you stand that place?" He asks, pointing to the entrance of Porta di Roma. "Thirty minutes? Forty?"

You say nothing. The longest you've ever managed was fifty-three, with bathroom breaks between one held breath and another.

"That stuff lowers resistance to the other 'psychosomatic' requests: acquisition anxiety, visual stimuli with 'on sale' and 'special offer' written across them, aural signals and light up signs, general chaos, hunting for the best deals, fear of being cheated, free samples outside the shop, smiling hostesses and a whole range of specially developed tactics ter push people inta buying, increasingly closer ter the limits of compulsiveness."

"Is that why you wear plants and flowers?"

"You gottit, personal defence. A few years ago, the heads of Porta de Roma decided ter get rid of the trees because of the insects they attracted, and look what they did," he says, pointing at the artificial plants ringing the edges of the forecourt. "Now only that one's left, poor bloody *Ailanthus*, the tree of *Paradise Lost*, but look what a state it's in, it's just a symbol, fenced in an' caged like an inmate of Rebibbia.[26]"

The Tree of Heaven sways weakly, pushed by a breath of autumn breeze, apparently confirming the man's judgement. Then the old man sniffs the air and wrinkles his nose. "Porta de Roma stinks . . . it ain't a simple collection of shops; it's a social experiment, like the Vatican City after the Lateran Treaty, with its guards, special laws, Sunday thoroughfare rights . . . they finished building it *before* the houses 'round here, not the other way 'round, with the shopping center supplying the demands of the neighborhood . . . who knows where the profits go or if they even pay taxes."

"I just wanted to buy a pair of panties."

"Panties, yeah? Maybe that's why . . . What's your name?"

"Elisa."

"My pleasure, I'm Corrado, but everyone calls me Colorado."

"Why?"

"I'll tell ya another time. Firs' though, if ya wanna come back in 'ere without problems, I gotta learn ya some *plant defence*."

PLASTIPOOPERS

Colorado's plant defences can't actually look you in the eye, but it's as if they are doing so through your nostrils. You appreciate their reservedness, you don't feel watched,

---

26 Rebibbia: Prison in Rome

and you can smell their presence, perceive their essence and exchange smells and perfumes with each as if it were the hint of a greeting or a mark of courtesy at a first meeting.

Colorado lives behind PuzzleLab in the Tufello area, you must have gone past it a thousand times on your way between home and uni, but you never ever noticed, until now, the overgrown patch of land hidden by a kind of hedge of brambles on Via di Monte Meta.

"Don't let it bother you, I know it looks like a mess, but it's natural."

A little round hut, a 3D resin print, is filled with flowerpots of all shapes and sizes holding plants, flowers and small trees. Every electronic object present in this space is paired with a plant to "purify" it: the TV screen on the wall is framed by the curved trunk of a very fleshy cactus defined by lines of long prickles, the fridge is set into the trunk of a cherry tree, the washing machine, on the other hand, is a spinning drum of fir wood connected to a chain and worked by a set of bamboo pedals.

"C'mon, ter the greenhouse."

Outside, in the garden, another more rudimentary tensile structure, about twenty meters long, is covered with flexible solar panels and dotted with little turbines whose flexible oval blades look like tulip petals. With any hint of a breeze, they start to spin, making a pleasant hissing sound, a kind of energzsing hum.

"Lemme introduce the countermeasures, or better, me tactical weapons."

If it weren't for the labels, you probably wouldn't recognize most of the numerous herbs: rosemary, sage, summer savory, fennel, marjoram, thyme, chamomile, lavender, Italian strawflower, garlic and plantains.

"What do you do?" You ask, curious.

"I could be a 'erbalist or a medic, but the work concept don't suit me, yeah. What about you? I bet you're still studyin', bet you're about twenty yeah?"

"Twenty-two, I moved here last year from Civitavecchia after years of commuting. I'm finishing my degree in Science of Communication at Tor Vergata, specializing in Semiotics."

"Ahaha, I specialize in *seediotics,*" Colorado bursts out laughing.

As well as the herbs there are some flowers with special names: a red rose called Pëtr Alekseevič Kropotkin in honor of the anarchic philosopher; a yellow carnation dedicated to the environmental activist Vandana Shiva; another, silver colored one, in honor of the agricultural hacker Pawel Ngei; and a heliotrope for the political militant Valerio Verbano.

"These roses are so beautiful!"

"Ahh, them's my girls. I made them."

"What do you mean?"

"I mean me old man taught me how ter manipulate stamen, corolla, petals, anthers, pistils, and ter cross breed species an' invert flower varieties. Took me six years ter grow these girls."

In just a few minutes you have realized that your knowledge of flowers is embarrassing; you would hardly be able to tell one from the other.

"Is it hard?"

"Difficult, nah. Tiring, yup. Hybridization has to be done before dawn, when the anthers ain't open yet. Then you take the male flowers, pull off 'is petals an' leave 'em on a piece of paper in the sun. When they're all dry the stamens open an' drop their pollen on the paper. After a few hours you collect it with a funnel an' scatter it on the female organs, an' fertilization is complete."

You are ashamed of your ignorance. You blush, lower your gaze and change the subject.

"So where do you keep your defences?"

"Over 'ere, lemme show you," he answers, showing you the way along the path. "Porta de Roma used ter be only fields, when I were a kid, I used ter go wiv me mum an' dad ter pick chicory and mint. Then when they started ter build, me mum and' dad started ter plant 'ere everything that would disappear from there. We was right an'all, if we 'adn't replanted I wouldn't 'ave anything ter eat now, I'd 'ave ter eat that artificial rubbish from the supermarket."

The plant defences are presented to you one by one through Colorado's tale. "'Ere they are . . . now introduce yourselves!"

You can see the labels written crisp and clear.

Mint - Colds, fever, respiratory disease, thoracic congestion.

Sage - Inflammation of the oral cavity, swollen stomach, small wounds, excessive sweating, menopausal disturbances.

Cardoon - Jaundice, bilious colic, hepatitis, stomach ache, ulcers, venous circulation deficiencies.

Passion Flower - Insomnia, gastrointestinal problems, generalized anxiety syndrome.

"Why do you label them? Who are they for?"

"Well, I don't do this all by meself. Once a week I open the greenhouse so whoever wants ter can come get what they need. The labels 'elp 'em find what they need without always asking me what's this for, what's that for . . ."

"Are these VOCs really so dangerous? I've never heard of them."

"'Course ya 'aven't, it ain't like they advertise 'em. Shops, offices an' apartment blocks contain a load of stuff derived from plastic an' they produce VOCs, like formaldehyde, benzene, xylene or trichloroethylene; stuff that's in glue, paint, pipes an' joints or adhesives an' furniture, especially veneers. If that stuff builds up in the air it can make you ill: asthma, coughing, catarrh. The Americans call it 'sick building syndrome.'"

Suddenly so many situations become clear to you: your nausea, dizziness and mood swings over recent months in Porta di Roma stick in your throat like acid reflux. The explanation doesn't make you feel any better. Then you are distracted by a movement.

"What are those for?"

You can see a handful of worms wiggling through the earth; they are squirming enthusiastically around a piece of polystyrene.

"I call them plastipoopers, they eat polystyrene. Ter start with they was beetle larva, of the *Tenebrio* genus, an' inside they have some microorganisms that allow 'em ter process plastic particles."

"Like carrier bags?" As you ask, a bad idea is already taking shape in your mind.

"Exactly, around fifty plastipoopers can convert 20 grams of polythene per day."

"What do they turn it in to?"

"Carbon dioxide, like they would any uvver food."

"I think I may have an idea, but first, could you make me a 'neutralizer?'"

"'Course, what d'ya need it for?"

"I have to go back to Porta di Roma. And I have to be able to stay there for at least an hour."

So, you return to your assault on the shopping center, you charge, eyes straight ahead, nostrils flaring, but this time you are full from head to toe with *Dracaena reflexa*, peace lily, *Epipremnum aureum*, *Philodendron*, ivy and *Chlorophytum*. Colorado prepared these botanic defences for you this morning at dawn after gathering bunches of fresh herbs in the greenhouse.

All your pockets are full of them, every hem stuffed, every buttonhole decorated.

You look funny, like a New Age jester, but you don't care, because in this amusing attire nobody will look at you with their usual scorn. Even your semiotics professor might judge you differently in light of the symbolism of the demonstrative action you are about to execute. Unfortunately, the backpack stuffed with bags of earth you are carrying is slowing you down, but you remain determined not to be stopped by any security guards and their tablets connected to the panoptic room.

From the entrance on the main concourse where the poor Tree of Heaven rises in its prison, you walk directly to the left toilet on the ground floor. You shut yourself in the bathroom for the time necessary to count and check the state of the bags of worms you and Colorado prepared together. You want to draw fluorescent blue graffiti on that horrible mosaic of rectangular grey tiles, but you have no time to lose over the ugliness of the interior design. As soon as you have finished counting you leave the bathroom, look around and drop a bag in each of the three rubbish bins by the entrance, and then head towards the next toilets.

On the online map of Porta di Roma, you counted four men's toilets and four women's on the ground floor, and the same on the first floor. There should be at least thirty-six more bins scattered throughout the corridors and numerous bars and food courts. You have faith in your physical endurance, not least because as you distribute the bags the weight on your shoulders diminishes, giving you back the strength and courage to carry out your mission of disturbance that could also improve the collective awareness of Porta di Roma's visitors.

The plastipoopers bring a message of deliverance and redemption from forced purchasing, from the daily purgatorial procession past shop windows, and against the rosary of consumerism that clicks by, week by week, until wages are cleaned out and monthly repayment rates begin. Just for once you would like to see the incredulous faces of people discovering the beauty of decay, the allure of bacterial digestion, the wonder of organic transformation. This illusory satisfaction is denied to you in the exact moment you step onto the escalator.

You realize too late—when you are two meters up and unable to turn back—you are leaking grains of earth from your backpack and the trail produced by the greed of the plastipoopers is making you identifiable to every CCTV camera in the shopping center. There, at the top of the escalator, is the security man again, waiting for you open-armed, tablet under tucked under his armpit, ready to throw you and your beloved maggots out.

You feel like crying, you could scream and stamp your feet, but you simply close your eyes and let him do what he has to do. Your seminary on 'applied semiotics' ends up down the toilet as if it were semolina.

As soon as your butt hits the ground under the *Ailanthus*, the security guard says, "You've really done it this time," waves the tablet in your face, and waits for the AGA to save your features to the cloud and its everlasting digital memory. "You're banned from Porta di Roma for the next three years."

HACK-EDEN

"Dammit, I'm useless. No good for anything." You lower your eyes and look at your trainers spattered with earth.

"Nah, you're wrong, you're good for sumfink for someone," says Colorado in an attempt to cheer you up.

"Who?"

"A group of friends. They're banned from the shoppin' center an'all. If you ain't got nuffink ter do, I'll take ya."

Any kind of distraction from how you're feeling now would be welcome. You nod uncertainly and Colorado winks at you. It doesn't take longer than 10 minutes on his electric tandem for you to cross Tufello and get to Vigne Nuove.

"See? It only took a moment," he says after letting you down to lock the bike to a lamppost. "Welcome ter Hack-Eden, or if you prefer, Hacker's Paradise."

Behind the beige buildings along Viale Ennio Flaiano there is an expanse of parked vehicles. Some no longer have tires, some have no windows or windscreens.

"Looks like a junkyard to me."

"Exactly, that's what the street drones see. They also suffer from 'plant blindness,' in practice they can only see what they recognize. An' the drones are programmed ter identify plates, not species of flora. Now take a better look."

As soon as you focus on the interiors, you begin to understand that in reality the cars are flower pots, and the bodies of the cars are shells, seats removed, to make it possible to cultivate hundreds of plants and vegetables inside them.

"In Milan they 'ave the vertical forest, we 'ave a botanic parking lot," says Colorado, laughing a big belly laugh without hiding a certain amount of pride. Then he is distracted by a few people coming towards them.

"Hey looky here! Colorado's back!" A slender young man with olive skin and arms tattooed to look like a biomechanical android holds out his hand first to Colorado, then to you in greeting.

"Pleased to meet you, I'm Senthil."

Behind him there are another three people carrying various gardening tools.

"Why do they call you Colorado?" You whisper the question this time.

"I'll tell ya anuvver time."

"Hey Colora', who have you brought us this time?" Asks a middle-aged woman wearing a camo overall. Her hair is coppery, and her face is lined like the bark of a stone pine.

"This is Elisa, she suffers from the same syndrome as we do, she needs to learn a bit of guerilla gardening."

"Ah, you're in the right place then. C'mon, I'll show ya the way," says Senthil, indicating to the road towards the parking lot. Colorado, on the other hand, stops to chat with the woman. The other two nod to you because their hands are full.

"Hi, I'm Yilun," says a woman of about forty with Oriental features and flowery dungarees.

"Pleased to meet you, my name's Pino," says a large man wearing a large pair of silvery augmented reality glasses.

As you wander through the rows of disused cars you notice solar panels installed on their roofs, the hiss of wind tulips mounted on the side mirrors, server LEDs glittering from slightly open trunks, and many ARDUINO boards, power cables and 3D printers.

"Over the last ten years," Senthil tells you, "cars ready to be scrapped have been 'donated' by the neighborhood people to our project of energy and food independence. They give us metals and we give them electricity and vegetables."

"What if you're discovered?"

"Nothing will happen. There are so many of us, two thousand families living off-grid across Tufello and Vigne Nuove. More botanic parking lots are sprouting up like wildfire in Casalina, Aurelio, Magliana, and Garbatella."[27]

---

27 Boroughs of Rome

"But won't they close the parking lots?"

"Even if they were to find the money to dismantle everything," he carries on pointing up, "we are ready with our gardentecture on the apartment blocks with hanging gardens on their balconies. They can't do anything about those. They wanted property to become private, didn't they?" Senthil says with a histrionic grin. "So for the moment, this is our Hacker's Paradise where we experiment with guerilla gardening tactics and strategies."

This is when you start to tell him about your failures, about your anger and frustration at being banned from Porta di Roma and your desire for revenge. For his part Senthil shows you how the "wood-wide-web"—the communication network between plants—works, the interspecies defence strategy known as "the enemy of my enemy is my friend," and the definitive weapon of plants, the so-called "retreat and burned earth" to prevent and dissuade the advance of any potential aggressor.

Your walk ends at four rubbish trucks whose cargo beds have been converted into nesting areas for the birds that pass through Rome in autumn as they migrate to warmer climes. Just then, you see hundreds of starlings swirling over the parking lot, as they swoop and twirl, dive and climb, and you have another moment of illumination, but this time you hold your tongue, say nothing and wait until you get to know the community of people with Gruen syndrome like you, better. You won't be able to do it on your own, you're going to need a lot of help to achieve your goal.

A Question of Synthesis

Within a few weeks you already know how to juggle neutralizing infusions and improvised botanic defences because you have learned to identify and gather at least two dozen kinds of herbs that grow alongside the sidewalksof Tufello. You have even installed an opensource geo-referenced map on your cell phone with which you move with agility from one plant to the next according to the needs of the day. You frequently commute between Colorado's solar greenhouse and the parking lot in Via Ennio Flaiano to give a hand where it is needed, but above all you have gotten to know your "guerilla comrades" better.

Olivia teaches biology at Sapienza University, and in her free time she is an herbalist. She believes eating flowers is healthy. It is a not very well-known tradition, only really used by starred chefs, but nevertheless probably dates back to the times of ancient Egypt. According to her, the idea that a flower isn't edible is wrong; after all, we eat artichokes, turnip tops and cauliflowers. "So why not roses?" says Olivia. "The petals are really tasty, I put them in pies."

Senthil studied agriculture in Viterbo, and after being a farmhand in Latina, he now works as a gardener. However, in his field he is known for having expanded and developed the network of urban kitchen gardens in northern Rome. He knows how to cook an infinite number of pestos with dozens of different spices.

Pino is an environmental journalist and communication sciences researcher in Roma Tre. He founded Freewalker, a cultural association that organizes walks to learn about the territory through "psychogeographical exploration" of the city. His expeditions are one of the activities most sought after by the university students (people say they have great trips!).

Yilun is a designer and land planner who moved from Beijing to Rome fifteen years ago for love. She discovered the "solartivism" current—a tool for analyzing reality at the crossroads between renewable energy, art, and activism—and since then she has been working on finding funding and grants to make the Via Ennio Flaiano parking lot a useful place for the neighborhood and an example to be copied elsewhere.[28] She takes care of the group's social media and PR.

So, during today's meeting you decide it's time to spill the beans.

"I'm going to lay out my strategy for you, in reality it's the synthesis of these last few weeks we've spent together. Perhaps, if things go well, it will also be the basis of my degree dissertation."

You stand and begin to draw the perimeter of Porta di Roma with a twig on the dusty ground by the parking lot, then you draw some diagonal lines that, from the exterior, converge on the center of the shopping center. You explain your plan down to the smallest detail, both stages 1 and 2. You watch the surprised expressions on your companions' faces, listen to all their doubts and objections and respond with other points and segments of the plan that you draw on the lower part of the diagram.

In the end, Olivia claps her hands and crows, "It's crazy! You're mad, but I like it, I'm in!"

"I might be mad, but I feel like that poor Tree of Heaven. Caged and treated like an unwanted weed to be kept at a distance for fear that I may corrupt the surrounding environment."

"Exactly," says Olivia, "the history of the *Ailanthus* is truly sad. First it was brought here from Asia, and then it was shunned. In the nineteenth century, when pébrine, a disease afflicting silkworms, became widespread, silk farmers decided to use another kind of Lepidoptera, the ailanthus silkmoth, in order to continue the production of silk. This

---

28 Solartivism is a neologism formed from the words "solar" and "activism."

species doesn't make silk as fine as that of the *Bombyx mori*, but it ended up being used in half of Europe."

"Then? Then what happened?" You ask as if this question hides the mystery of your own genealogy.

"Then they found a cure for pébrine and the domestic silkworm regained its place on the mulberry tree, leaving the ailanthus silkmoth to sink into oblivion. Worse, nowadays the Tree of Heaven is seen as an unwanted weed to uproot and eradicate."

"But it hasn't vanished."

"No, luckily a number of specimens of the ailanthus moth escaped the farms and reproduced on *Ailanthus* trees that in the meantime had been planted to strengthen railway embankments, or along tree-lined avenues and as anti-erosion measures throughout the territory."

"They shouldn't be so badly treated," says Senthil.

"Of course, if a plant is looked after in a garden, it is called exotic, if it grows on its own, taken there by the wind, it's thought of as a weed. The same plant can be both welcomed and clandestine."

"A bit like with people," Yilun adds.

"Yes, though for plants, a garden is like an enclosure."

"And for people a nation is an enclosure," you burst out, "so long live intermixture!" You look at your guerilla comrades one by one, and hold their experienced, slightly tattered, gazes despite being the youngest and newest arrival. "So, are you going to give me a hand or what?"

Colorado lifts a hand, and you hurry to slap it with enthusiasm. Olivia, Senthil, Pino and Yilun do the same.

OPERATION GUANOPOCALYPSE
You look at the sky over Porta di Roma knowing your revenge will come soon.

The clouds of starlings thicken and stretch like cotton-wool clouds in spring, light grey, joyous, cinematographic, and totally innocuous. Only today it is Christmas day, and those starlings are one of the elements of a malicious gift you are about to offer the shopping center customers as a form of compensation for everything that has happened over the last few months. Snickers. Reports. Questioning. Isolation. Pushing and shoving. Humiliation.

Now you know that the enemy of your enemy may be your friend.

Now you know that plants and their rhizosphere may become a defence at the same time as being salvation for a decadent society.

Porta di Roma is three hundred meters as the crow flies from Olivia's house. Your guerilla comrades, like troops before going into battle, have deployed in reconnaissance while you, captain but forbidden from taking part in person, direct manoeuvres from a distance.

"It's on. The delivery riders have confirmed," you tell the others with a voice message over Telegram. Using Olivia's birdwatching binoculars, you study the swarming customers hurrying to buy last-minute presents before the ceasefire for Christmas dinner. Lines of consumers in queues, double lines of cars heavy on their horns, flocks of mopeds, families clearly in the grip of desires beyond their budgets and couples anxious to finish the day with a glorious relationship-saving economy buy.

Thumbs up from your comrades appear in the Telegram chat, so you move your gaze to the forecourt. You smile at the poor *Ailanthus*—you're doing this for the tree too, in a way —then you begin to notice the first splashes appear on the cobblestones: a continuous splattering which within a few minutes leaves the forecourt looking speckled. You can't hear the sounds nor smell the odors, but you know what is about to happen. The paving transforms, changing color from greyish-brown to yellowy-green as what people at first thought (and hoped) was just a kind of cleaning treatment for the hygiene of the outdoor environment, turns out to be a layer of viscid guano...

Realizing that there are flocks of starlings swirling above them, people look with horror into the air and attempt to protect themselves with gift boxes, using designer shopping bags as shields and hiding under gift wrappings, but a slew of liquid effluence rains down on them from above. All because the birds are greedy for a compote made of creamed olives and sugary fruit you have prepared in large quantities over the last few days.

The first stage of the plan has begun, it would not have worked without the birds or trees in the right positions. You had the starlings ready to take off from the parking lotin Via Ennio Flaiano, but to guide them all the way to Porta di Roma on the right day you had to rely on all the experience and knowledge of your guerilla comrades: seeing as the shopping center has had every plant and tree removed, you asked Bharathi—Senthil's brother who runs the children's entertainment park—to suggest an inflatable forest by the parking lot entrances as a Christmas attraction. This would provide the birds with a place to spend the night before the mission. To make the starlings roost in the right place, the inflatables were spread with your compote by the technicians who put them up, all delivery rider friends of Colorado and assiduous visitors to the Puzzle-Lab social center.

In the meantime, the situation on the forecourt has got worse and the thin film of guano has become a thick, insidious membrane that hundreds of people are slipping and sliding on, while a similar number of cars skate and skid dangerously on it too.

"Are the plastipoopers ready?" You ask the chat.

"Yup, baskets open," Senthil answers, he and Pino are responsible for carrying out what you didn't manage to finish yourself a few months ago.

The security agents are in turmoil, they have never had to face an enemy like this, so many and so anonymous, nor have they ever had to pilot the drones to disperse hundreds of starlings. When the first drone hits one of the inflatables, it makes a hole in it, causing a boom like a tire bursting and the ensuing chaos spreads everywhere. In a frenzy of fear the birds push other drones into the plastic trees which split and burst one after the other. Then, thousands of more people pour out of Porta di Roma's exits gripped by horror: the sight of the plastipoopers has pushed them to run out to the parking lots. Some seek refuge in their cars, some open umbrellas and others sacrifice their designer boxes in order to open a path through the panicking crowd.

You watch all this calmly, and when you see mushroom canopies—the spores of which were spread carefully over the interstices in the parking lot paving in readiness for this day—pushing through the cracked asphalt, you know the first stage of your plan has been successfully completed.

Walking and driving have become a repellent, disgusting, but extremely aware experience. In a very short time, the fleeing cars are covered in guano and causing traffic-jams and accidents causing a gridlock right up to the beltway.

"Retreat. Mission accomplished," you type into the chat in satisfaction.

SIX MONTHS LATER
EVERYTHING HAS BEEN CONSUMED.

For over two months, thanks to Yilun's hard work, the hashtag #guanopocalypse has been one of the most commented themes on the social networks. The interminable stream of posts, pictures and videos recorded over Christmas Eve has been enough to decree the slow but sure decline of Porto di Roma.

The second stage of the plan, in fact, consists of waiting. The danger of the starlings, plastipoopers and mushrooms returning has pushed customers to less risky shopping venues.

After the third month of free-falling profits, Porta di Roma's Board of Directors, in a plenary online meeting covering nine time zones, approves a motion proposing "investments be temporarily suspended in view of the appropriate legal action, tax relief and financial support the Lazio region will have to implement in order to restore favorable conditions for the valorization activities of the Porta di Roma area."

Nobody has so far suspected a link between the birds, inflatables and the compote.

Nobody noticed your guerrilla comrades hanging around Porta di Roma over the days preceding Christmas Eve: every CCTV camera was moved just enough to create "invisible corridors" hard to notice from the control room.

Four months later, when the service, maintenance and security personnel's contracts were up, what happened during the Covid-19 pandemic does so again at Porta di Roma; the disappearance of the last of the staff leaves the space free for other species, despite some hardcore shoppers still wandering around the almost derelict shops forced into a relentless "everything must go."

Five months later, graffiti starts appearing and broken windows aren't fixed. The birds—now that there is no more light or sound pollution—have begun to nest on the roofs, and a vigorous grassy mantle, wild and unmanicured, has spread up the escalators and covered the internal terraces and part of the floor on the second story. Instead of drones, elegant brown *Bombyx*, large moths of about fifteen centimeters, have started to fly and feed on the *Ailanthus* leaves. Pino and Senthil have reintroduced them to this habitat that has mutated to their advantage without too much trouble.

As has become habitual for you and Colorado over the last few months, you arrive in the forecourt on his tandem. The concourse is now more like a clearing. After riding along the whole connecting route between Tufello and Porta di Roma, you find Olivia, Senthil, Pino and Yilun waiting for you, tools in hand. Before anything else, you greet the Pantocrator *Ailanthus*, whose seeds—known as samara—have finally found cracks and crevices to germinate in, thanks to the work the mushrooms did to disturb the cobblestones leading to the entrances of IKEA and LEROY MERLIN.

"My degree dissertation is nearly ready. Come, let's go inside."

Plumbago auriculata, a large cloud of blue flowers, cascades down the walls of the ex-Porta di Roma, and where a few months previously the illuminated banners of EXTYN and JONNY JOY were planted, huge purple artichoke flowers bloom. The colorful neon lights of IDEXE and flashing sequences of OKAIDI have been replaced with thick swarms of bees buzzing around on the hunt for flowers to drink from. The fluo-halo of the PIMKIE shop window can still be seen between three and four o'clock in the afternoon when the sun passes over the broken skylight. The tower of rotting fliers in the supermarket is home to an ant's nest and there are goldfinches nesting in the SONNY BONO satellite speakers.

"It's wonderful, everything has been consumed," you say, walking along the central corridor.

The group stops in front of H&M's window.

"It was the only shop whose window was still in one piece."

Two cell phones mounted on wooden stands are filming the display space behind the shop window.

"Because we live in artificial times measured out by electronic devices and digital algorithms," you say to your comrades as if you are about to do a rehearsal for your degree dissertation, "our attention has adapted to the scale of a nanosecond and the breadth of a beam of light. We are losing our ability to think 'to' and 'with' other living beings and natural processes that exist on different temporal and geographical scales: the changing seasons, bird migration, the lifespans of trees and plants."

In the shop window a number of *Ailanthus* saplings are "nutating," that is, moving in the manner typical of plants inside a collection of post-apocalyptic-style clothes, and it really looks like they are wearing them. A poem has been sprayed in electric yellow paint on the right-hand window.

> *I like to think (right now, please!) of*
> *a cybernetic forest filled with pines and electronics*
> *where deer stroll peacefully*
> *past computers*
> *as if they were flowers*
> *with spinning blossoms.*
> Richard Brautigan (All Watched Over by Machines of Loving Grace)

The installation is complete when you start the video of the last three weeks at 5x speed.

"However, our attention span is something orientable, trainable, something that can be trained to an 'enhanced,' more-than-human speed. Data collection, measurement, recording and phenomena visualization tools can be used to increase awareness and develop a different capacity for attention and care, especially if we are able to make conscious choices regarding the type and quality of time(s) in which we want to live."

The start of the video shows shoots breaking through the ground and starting to "circumnutate," moving as they rise up and grow in an irregular circle or ellipse. Nutation is what allows leaves to fold and flatten, petals to wrinkle and curl: this mechanism is at the root of almost all plant movement, and after days and days has modeled the clothes in a way not necessarily similar to human anatomy.

"The problem is this: we human beings occupy such a slim slice of time and space that we cannot imagine the speed and scale of other worlds, we cannot think at their pace or understand the changes we have forced on them, nor how we must adapt in order to all survive. Our minds alone are not capable of this task, but thanks to technology and imagination that, combined, give rise to a kind of real science fiction, we possess the right tools to correct our biological limits."

In front of your guerrilla comrades, a slice of the life of the *Ailanthus* trees is taking shape, the dynamism intrinsic in their fluid movements caused by desire and fear is immediately clear.

Ten minutes into the video, the nutators are wearing the clothes and have taken on a bizarre hybrid identity, which despite everything is surprisingly close to our world.

"Nutation can be seen in every plant, from sunflower seedlings to beech trees, from mushrooms to the hyphae of mycelia. Life is awakened and launches on a hunt and exploration of their surroundings and the start of an incredible adventure," you conclude and take a small bow next to the nutators, who appear to copy you.

Your guerrilla comrades applaud: Olivia is clearly moved, Colorado is visibly concentrating, Senthil gives you a thumbs up and Pino is smiling broadly and bursts out with, "I propose honors and an academic kiss!"

They come in for a group hug and kiss your cheeks and forehead. You finally feel like part of something without borders, something undefinable, impossible to explain in words. You feel their arms around you and at the same time see a number of branches pushing against the glass. The buds have left some marks, light opaque tracks left by nutation. Perhaps it is their language, a form of communication using the tips of their twigs, not unlike our own manual communication. This mystery reminds you of another, so you take Colorado to one side.

"Are you ready yet to tell me why they call you Colorado?"

He grins and this time humors you.

"My father was a biologist an' wanted to get back ter the land because he was fed up wiv eating supermarket food. When he were thirty he went to America for three months for work an' pleasure. He wanted to bring back to Italy certain plants suitable for arid terrain. He believed climate change was coming more quickly an' severely than anyone was saying on TV. When he brought back the plants, he even brought back my mother."

"Your mother? How do you mean?"

"I mean she was working as a character in one of those sad theme parks showing 'ow Native Americans used to live."

"Was she Native American?"

"Yup, can't you see it?"

"Well, with your accent I thought you looked like you were probably from somewhere in southern Italy."

"That's partially true, me father's name were De Stefano and came from Sicily, but my mother were a Cherokee of the Culstee family, from Colorado."

"We all migrate, animals, plants and people."

Senthil comes over to them and asks, "We've been here over an hour, how do you feel?"

"Great, I hadn't even noticed the time passing."

You look at your dirty hands, covered in earth, pollen and who knows how many microbes. We look at you with gratitude, as we have from the start, telling this story from our privileged point of view, from every pore and bacterium of your organism. Because we all live together, even if we can't all be seen.

Today yet another artificial tree appeared in front of my balcony. I am living surrounded by a small forest of plastic plants, I am overshadowed by their hulking forms. They were erected in a night to improve 5G reception in the neighborhood! Instead of the blue sky and white clouds through my windows there is only grey concrete. I can now also hear the rustling of plastic plane trees without knowing whether the sound emitted from the leaf speakers is being transmitted live from some forest in the Trentino area or if it is a squalid recording of when there used to be a copse of pine trees by my house.

This time the frondy fake is shorter than three meters. If I needed to, I could use it as a fire escape. The TV pylon covered in fake pine needles is already next to it, as is a line of electricity pylons wearing terrible brown carpet to disguise them.

A studio apartment on the fourth of sixteen floors can't disperse that much stress so I decide to go out to clear my brain. As I go to the door, the prototypes of noses, ears and fingers stare anxiously at me from the shelf next to the Chemical Brothers poster. I have to deliver two samples of noses and three of ears to the burn unit at Sant'Eugenio hospital by Monday morning; however, until I have calmed down, I would only manage to damage the 3D printer. Always assuming the seasonal blackouts don't prevent me from composing during the weekend.

Outside I look for small gatherings of people, mounds of sweating flesh and concentrations of human odors. At least until the plastiplane trees are able to diffuse synthetic odors to fool our senses. I can't see a living being. A drone here and there doing remote sightseeing for who knows who, who knows where. The odd self-driving car wanders around aimlessly waiting for passengers to wake up their sensors. The only food delivery riders to be seen are agile dog-like things piloted remotely by gamers sprawled on sofas to earn a few bucks to get their latest upgrade.

Then I see them, standing in the shade of a spiral staircase behind the shopping center. There are at least eight of them, adolescents between twelve and thirteen. Their excitement shows as they fiddle with their phones, sending symphonies of emoticons. I move closer after sending a warning string: peace sign + hands up + smile + shy.

They answer with a line of thumbs up. Bro + Bro + Bro.

One of them moves aside and there, in the middle of them, I spot a woman on her knees wearing the orange uniform of a "livecatcher." Pest control officers are called in for getting rid of bugs and rats, but they deal with all kinds of things now though: wolves, wild pigs, foxes, rabbits, tortoises, squirrels, otters and swallows.

The object they are staring at, almost as if it were a heavenly vision, is a light-emitting phenomenon, it looks as if dozens of LEDs have been strung in line, or as if a rainbow has been reduced to lines laid out on the ground. The emoticons scroll as fast as can be: question marks, exclamation marks, surprised faces, perplexed hands and bizarre animals, everything a keyboard can provide.

In the end, the expert—probably a zoologist, in my opinion—after snatching up the creature with a litter grabber from the drain, emits a verdict: VIPER.

Everybody suddenly takes a step back. The emoticons become prohibition signs, running legs, butterfly nets, poison, jars, bars, cages, hand grenades and atomic mushroom clouds.

I want to see that glow up close. It looks artificial but it isn't.

"It isn't dangerous," she says, turning to the kids, but there is only me, because the kids have already vanished, gone off to look for other signals to capture on their screens. "It's just scared."

Then, pushing a little on a lump under the reptile's jaw she pulls a rat out of its mouth.

"Why is it fluorescent? I thought that only happened to insects?" I say, curiously.

"Yes, but not just them. It is chemiluminescence, it means this poor beast has been modified, or it has developed some new traits for surviving in the city. I'll have to analyze its DNA to answer your question."

"What're you going to do with it?"

"I'm going to take it to the reptile tank. There are another two there, and this certainly won't be the last. It'll be safe there and won't be lonely."

The fluorescent glimmer disappears into the zoologist's backpack, but stays stuck in my mind.

That night all sorts happen: I dream fluo dreams with fluo people dancing in fluo clothes, on fluo limbs and pieces composed on the 3D printer, like wings, feelers, fins, claws, crests and tails. Fluo me, dancing with them too. Then I eat fluo, drink fluo, and secrete fluo. It is all fluo within fluo that fluos in a continuous flow. In the end I fluo myself and when I wake up and through the window can only see the copse of plastic trees, antennas disguised as luxuriant plants, green and yellow neon-framed hoardings and synthetic climbing plants reaching right across my windowsill, I come to a realization.

I give my instructions to ChatGPT and within ten minutes download two VR tutorials and a video: the first, by a bioengineer from MIT in Boston, is about how phosphorescence works (instructive but complicated and therefore useless); the second, from Bangalore, is about the photophore organs of a snail (valuable for discovering luciferin (an organic substance present in luminescent organisms) in the presence of ATP, magnesium and the luciferase enzyme loses electrons and frees energy as light); and the video is of a man from near Civitavecchia with a swimming pool full of fluorescent orange krill he sells at children's parties.

Then I open the nanoCAD software and input the snail luceferin formula: it's a long-chain aldehyde and a reduced riboflavin phosphate. Then, on the open-source site e-Den, I buy the chemical formula of some commonplace seeds: clover, calendula, lemon, four o'clock and alfalfa. Then I hunt through the cartridges of organic materials I usually use for anatomical prostheses to see if I have the elements the nanoCAD needs. Just to be sure, I do a compatibility test. I would rather avoid any unpleasant surprises. I override the amber warnings by modifying a number of nutritional parameters of the original stem cells. Then I input the sequence of the photophore compound within the DNA of the seeds (the CRISPR-CasX plug-in shows me the exact location along the molecular string where I am most likely to have success) and press start.

I print a seed.

I feel like Pan, an enhanced wandering god of the forest.

Then I print another twenty, forty, eighty.

Until I come to the end of the ribbon of organic material.

In the grip of my excitement, I gather those grains of domestic technology and put them in a maize-plastic bag. Then I fill a basin with three cups of compost, five cups of clay and two of water. I use this mixture to make lots of little balls, as round as possible, and I press a seed into each one. As soon as I have finished filling all of the pockets in my botanical artillery jacket, I leave the house and jump on my scooter.

My seed sowing mission lasts until the sun goes down on the desolate streets: I dip my hands in my pockets and throw balls at random, without any specific targets, carrying out a joyous "seed-bombing" over every kilometer from my house to the beltway and back again. They call it guerrilla gardening, for me it is "wildocracy."

Where technology disguises nature, I want to naturalize technology—or technologize nature, I'll have to think about that.

I wait a couple of days, a couple of weeks, a couple of months. It doesn't rain and I turn into Pan-demon. I curse against the Capitalocene, against the extinction of the clouds, against plant blindness.

Dancing in a ring isn't enough, putting our hands together in prayer isn't enough, nor is invoking Gea, Pachamama, Žemyna, Tellus or Gaia. Insufflating the sky with silver iodide isn't enough.

Every day, along the route to Sant'Eugenio I scour the roads I have sewn in search of premonitory signs.

A sparrow planing in to peck.

A rabbit escaping in fear.

The telltale footsteps of a wild pig.

Nothing, my botanic bombs remain unexploded. Perhaps I used the wrong tutorial, perhaps I got the formula wrong, perhaps I got the dream wrong.

Every day my noses come out a little more crooked, the ears a little less perfect.

Every night I go home without fluo.

That's when the bad thoughts start: if my department supervisor notices these defects and complains about the quality of my prints, I risk going back to working as a groomer at the pet washing store H24, or worse still, becoming a crazy modder for the creative surgery clinic STRANIMALS. I have already printed far too many forked tails, fringed wings, Roman noses, elf-like ears, hooves with heels, hairless skins and retractable claws on those poor creatures.

Then, one morning, like so many avenging angels, amidst the branching domestic antennas, satellite dishes and air-conditioning engines, dozens of dark clouds appear. A false ceiling of angry meteorological agents grumble their disappointment and promise battle. I imagine them absorbing thousands of iridescent colors to then throw down a kaleidoscope of pouring rain, bolts of lightning and whirlwinds. May they uproot every signpost from its foundation, knock down the plastiplane trees and all their latest generation imitators and free us from the fabric of artificial scars infesting the urban landscape.

I go out on the balcony to celebrate a catastrophic but propitious event: raindrops make me wet, they soak me, they feed me. Everywhere within the range of my seeding action the first glowing shoots will be pushing through the earth, raising their timid little heads to illuminate the sidewalks and restore a beneficial glow to the asphalt necrosis, unaware of any of it.

Ecolution is coming this way, through free interspecies hybridization, through radical acts of imagination and through the occupation of ecological niches abandoned by the metastasis of gentrification.

In the middle of this deluge of water, I blink my eyes and see the brilliance. I see fluo even where there is none. Even darting flies create a fluo-tinted effect on my retinas. Perhaps it is a guided premonition, one scintillating color after another, one heavy shower after another. Lightning rages, drawing a cathartic cage and ionizing the air.

I hear a crack of lightning hit near me and am blinded. I cheer, perhaps this is the moment? I reopen my eyes and the plastiplane tree of torture wavers, leans and in the end, falls with a thunderous crash. Before permanently interrupting its transmission, the masked monster crashes into my building, destroys the railings on the balcony and rips away half of the floor, leaving me smiling and stunned on the edge of the fourth floor.

"What a disaster . . ." says the condominium park technician the next day.

I would like to answer "It's wonderful," but he might misunderstand my words.

"I don't think it can be repaired," I add mischievously, in an attempt to plant the seed of a terminal solution to the problem.

"What do you mean? . . . It's dangerous, it can't stay here like this."

"Well then, you could take it away, couldn't you?"

He looks at me like a cat watching reality TV. "Don't you want your balcony anymore?"

That's when I realize the extent of the abyss dividing us. I could give him a pair of better ears to help him better understand the urgency of what I mean, or perhaps a more powerful nose to smell the change that is happening. In the end, I don't answer; I escape.

I've called it "greenglimmer." It is my very own personal chlorophyllian fluo, the colour I spliced into the DNA of the seeds I planted. It incorporates the warmth of emerald green, the intense glow of saffron yellow, a dash of cobalt blue, plus something indefinable, perhaps indescribable, you have to see it to experience the fluoness.

It grows up from below and, like a subterranean dawn, lights the street, illuminates the facades of buildings and combats shadows and unwelcome timid presences. I crouch in front of the crack running from the road surface to the sidewalk and daydream . . . When the shoots turn green we will be able to walk through forests of tall trees as high as ten, twenty meters, or along walkways bordered by thick, luxuriant hedges, and when the plants open their iridescent canopies and stretch out like luminous brambles freeing themselves of any squalid artificial imitations, they will be our only source of fluo, capable of eliminating our lethal dependence on fossil fuels. We will go back in time and throw ourselves into the future . . .

I am contemplating my creatures close up, only a few centimeters away, crouched down by a wonderful crack in the pavement. None of the noses, eyelashes or lips I have made have ever done this to me. The idyll is interrupted as soon as I hear them arriving, preceded by their jingles and emoticons: doubt + strange + incredulity + radioactive + vomit + acid + alien invasion!

The influencers of the post-apocalypse first exchange photos of my creatures and then share them, feeding them to some post-pandemic algorithm, a health-hygiene panoptical guardian connected to a global cloud. They don't know what they are doing: their screens are the eyes of the basilisk, their microphones its ears, their emojis its synthetic tongue. In the digital reduction of emotive communication all the sophisticated grammar of my strategy of liberation is reduced to a single concept: danger!

Then danger becomes alarm, alarm emergency, and emergency a spontaneous reaction, as illogical as immediate as soon as my greenglimmer is mistaken for the usual alien glow. The reinforcements arrive, bigger and nastier than the kids. The truncheon brothers don't even introduce themselves before landing blows on my arms, my legs and my back. I fall to the ground curling into a ball, this time the fluo hurts—biting fluo flies, explosions, flashes and stars bursting everywhere—until, swollen and aching like any non-conforming thing, I stare at the greenglimmer with my cheek to the ground. We both know what being beaten and trampled means.

Looking out of their windows, people without faces or voices record footage of the assault, kick-starting memory memes. But they don't speak, they don't take sides, they don't defend me, they don't become indignant, but neither do they join in the beating. I don't know how to interpret this mass indifference. The lines of separation between complicity and fear, between aiding and abetting and indifference vanish, like intimate contour lines that vary from stomach to stomach.

Twenty seconds later, the neighborhood surveillance drones reach the pool of blood and greenglimmer where I am lying defenceless. The notifications launched by the little cowards evaporate in the distance along with the vulgar echoes of the truncheon brothers. Then, a tinny voice tells me to raise my hands. I want to obey, but I only manage to straighten my arms and stretch out along the ground.

The scan comes quickly, as does the sentence: the unexploded bombs in the pockets of my jacket nail me to the crime: provocation of alarm, environmental damage, eco-terrorism! A chain of crimes appears before me as soon as the operator releases the words from the drone like dropping an axe, "Don't move, you are under arrest!"

As it speaks, the drone drops a bio-containment stretcher to the ground. It opens like origami.

"Enter now and lie down, do not resist."

I am in for a treat: sterilization against pathogens, antiviral scanning and antibacterial isolation.

It is hard to imagine the scene from behind the bars of my cell.

During the first three months of my detention, (an AI sentenced me to a year plus a 3,000 euro reparation fine for environmental damage) teams of biological mine sweepers and ecological restorers will be eliminating all presence of greenglimmer with the excuse of public safety and possible alien species invasion.

In the following months, the first thing that the town authorities, scared by this mysterious entity, will have done is rope off every contaminated square meter with "defluorized area" signs, and then they will have concreted over every single plot of land, changing the designated use to make a parking lotor an area for construction.

I haven't lost hope, but it is hard without the grennglimmer, my way out of "in here" to "out there," from artificial reality, from forced reclusion. The prison is equipped with automatic dispensing machines, streaming on demand and animatronic pets, which help us to not completely lose our humanity (even though using an android to help with this matter is a paradoxical compromise).

Huge lights move rhythmically across the yard like they would a dance floor, making rainbow sequences skip across on the ground, partially to help the inmates' memories, and partially to keep our muscles in training (rather useful, actually, but above, in the cabins, there are prison guards with tasers and pistols in their belts, not DJs). In any case, every

Wednesday, when I am allowed out for an hour of air (not on the dance floor but in a yard where we are given VR visors), I notice something special. As I take the visor off to return it to its container, the shoes of one of the guards catches my eye . . . and I discover that Wednesday is fluo! Fluo like the electric-purple socks the officer is wearing under the trousers of his uniform. Maybe I am wrong, maybe it just my fluoro-mania, but it helps to keep me from going crazy and to not defluorize before I get out of here.

To pass the time, I have felt-tip pens delivered to me, fluorescent, obviously. When Officer Fluo comes into my cell and brings me what I asked for, I think he winks, and I have a "Tyler Durden" moment of glorious fluorophania.

I imagine I am not alone.

I imagine greenglimmer has survived eradication.

I imagine it is waiting for me to come back.

For twelve months I have asked for the lights in my cell not to be switched on. A wonderful, though pale imitation greenglimmer has spread all over the walls of my prison, every centimeter of space has been decorated with fluo pens. Now it is a more liveable and welcoming space because it has shades of color that, though natural, are often excluded or even actually banned from the urban agglomerates because they are considered strange and alien to the human idea— too human—of nature, (just look at cyanobacteria, jellyfish, fungal hyphae).

I have covered the walls with influorescence, the floor, too. I have drawn bundles of bacterial fluora meters long, and a mycopoietic mandala to decorate the ceiling above my head. I'm almost sorry to leave this work of fluorist art, because apart from the greenglimmer, I don't know what's waiting for me out there. Out of work, with no home (my rent contract expires in a month), I have no present, and my future looks like a patch of greenglimmer on the asphalt at the mercy of unknown forces.

"Are you ready?" Asks Officer Fluo, looking into my cell. I nod, I've been ready since I got here.

He opens the door and accompanies me to the exit to give me back my life.

We pass the canteen with its automatic dispensing machines and the rainbow dance floor of the yard. At the exit I collect my things. Officer Fluo winks at me again once more before I leave.

I take one step out of the prison gates, and I am swaddled by an orange mist. I wasn't expecting a welcoming committee. Looking around, there's not a living soul in sight. This surprise has made me ecstatic; it seems too good to be true that a "relative" of greenglimmer should have organized a welcome home party . . . but my eyes have deceived me, there is nothing fluorescent about this anonymous curtain of smoke. My nose tells me it's from an ordinary old rubbish pyre, piles of garbage incinerated and offered by the people as a propitiatory sacrifice to combustion and the benevolence of the deities of the Brand. This is not my ecolutional cycle.

I set off towards home. It's going to take hours.

The streets have changed. They are still victims of the heatwave; they look like they are about to crack and the asphalt to melt. My neighborhood hasn't changed either—shutters down, streets with the odd automatic street food rickshaw or print-everything tinker—until in the distance I see the buildings on my road, lit in a different way from how I remember.

As I get closer, a feeling of stunned wonderment grows within me, step after step: the videos and photos of my beating, after ending up online, have had an incredible effect. Not all of my neighbours live inside the splendid virtual lie for which the only imperative is fun, some have had the courage to welcome greenglimmer into their lives. These people saw the wonder of greenglimmer and understood it. Some must have gathered the shoots, taken them home and planted them in pots. The greenglimmer repaid this hospitality by generating an incredible iridescent effect capable of lighting the hallways, rooms and balconies.

Hundreds of apartments appear to be filled with aurora borealis. The luminosity is more or less constant, though sometimes it changes and varies according to the glow and type of greenglimmer.

I slip through my block's main door and hurry up the stairs, two steps at a time, to avoid uncomfortable questions like, "Where have you been all this time?", "When are you going to make me another nose?" and "Been on vacation have you, then?"

There is a registered mail letter on my doorstep. Opening the letter, I find that the condominium AI has notified me of the termination of my contract.

I go in, throw away noses, lips and ears, and head to where the balcony used to be.

With my feet hanging over the edge, I let my imagination run away with me: I dream of global air contamination, a fluodemic carried by pollen, spores and bacteria.

As soon as the sun goes down, I see a couple on the third-floor watering their plants. They look up towards me and give me a nod of thanks. Not long later, the intensity of the greenglimmer increases until it spreads all over the place, from thousands of windows all over the neighborhood. I am dazzled by my fluorescence joining the colors of an incandescent sunset.

The old is dead, the new has not yet managed to see the light of day…we need radical novums that resist the degradation and commodification of people and nature - Darko Suvin

NANOSOMES

Every time Shi goes back to China, she feels like she is leaping into the future. She last came four years ago so she is expecting a culture shock.

Through the car window—it is, of course, a self-driving car—she can see hundreds of huge, shiny residential buildings rising above the urban undergrowth of printable food stalls and the chaos of people running, walking, always online and rushing by. Three meters above the crowds, there are dozens of surveillance drones following kids and the elderly. Plumes of steam from automatic woks rise up here and there along the street, bluish in the light reflected from the screens held by their customers waiting for orders to be prepared.

"Food used to be just food," Shi thinks, remembering her father's words. "Then it turned into data, and now food and that data, in the form of algorithms and nanotechnology, are inextricably linked."

The city of Chongqing is like an urban membrane with tentacles spreading across dozens of hills, a tangle of streets and people impossible to unravel and separate. An enthralling knot where pollution has vanished. The hovering orange cloud blocking out the sun's rays is no longer there; in its place a dense, damp mist comes down at night and dissipates like a daily theater curtain come morning.

Shi's telephone vibrates and she connects it to the car's deck.

"Dad, I've just landed in Jiangbei. I was going to call you from the bus . . . How are you?"

The hologram shows an old man lying on his bed. Her father is wearing an oxygen mask over his face to help him breathe. His condition has taken a turn over the last few days.

"I've had worse days, don't worry. So, have you missed China? It's not like being in Italy, huh?"

"You know my roots are here."

Nearer to the bus station the density of market stalls and sellbots along the pavement increases; funny little androids serve bowls of steaming rice noodles in miso and douse them with a spicy red oil, then they add minced pork and top off the whole thing with pickles and peanuts. The customers are crowded together on tiny stools or around plastic tables.

Her father's eyes are half-closed, and someone is re-positioning his pillow. The young lady peers at Shi through the hologram, "Hi Shi, Maestro Ming is very tired now. He wanted to see you straight away, but it's better if rests now."

"I get it, Yun. Thank you for looking after him. I'll be there in about 4 hours."

Images from reality shows and cartoons run across the sides of the buildings, interrupted regularly by news flashes: the rural regeneration policies are broadcast everywhere, a stimulus to return home that is mobilizing millions of people.

Investors and lawyers explain the incentives and tax breaks connected to a return to one's ancestral home, which often coincides with the *hukou*, the place where their families are registered. The fight against urbanization has been going on for years, making the countryside more attractive: the numbers are exorbitant and impact the 45% of the Chinese population that has not yet moved to the cities, meaning about 10% of the world's population.

Shi gets out of the car in the station forecourt, flashes her screen at the android manning the entrance turnstile, crosses the waiting room and passes the ticket office that has been closed for years, and gets on the bus for Kaili.

For dozens of tunnels, the man in the opposite seat talks to her exclusively about work: BITING BYTES should collect its used cooking oil, instead of throwing it away after frying, because there is liquid gold in that waste oil, and if it could be put back into circulation it would levitate the profits of their 1,546 restaurants.

A serving robot goes backwards and forwards every thirty minutes along the corridor with hot tea and snacks displayed in its open chest. It talks too much, losing the thread in boring, rambling descriptions, making the journey a nightmare of advertizing. The oil drainage man talks non-stop about his culinary incidents: he has tried everything from filtering to combustion, from centrifuging to separation, from mixtures to additives, and now he is going to try with nanotechnology.

On hearing that word, Shi mists the window with her breath and draws a circle with an antenna at the top and two little arms holding on to the little arms of other circles. Then she pulls her hair back into a braid and tries to sleep. Just as she is dropping off, she remembers her father's designs and the incredible formulas that had taken him to work in Italy, where she was born and raised. Then, a few years ago, he had felt the call of his homeland and gone back to his village.

The circles start running through her dream; they come together, create links, make molecular bonds and aggregate, giving life to true cells—nanosomes—as Ming called them, when he tried to explain to her what he was doing.

"Are they like the invisible insects in rugs?" Little Shi had asked her father.

"Do you mean dust mites? They are a bit different, and they don't carry diseases. Actually, they are more like genes, like chromosomes, but I have improved them through observing nature."

"Why? Aren't our genes good enough?"

"Oh no, they are fine, it's just that they make us do some not very smart things sometimes."

"Like what?"

"Like, for example, the way we eat."

LANGDEZHEN

Three hours and fifty-five kilometers later, Shi wakes up in Kaili in Guizhou Province.

What had once been a village had become a TAO-BAO with crowded streets and pervasive urban farming. Thanks to rural development policies, the mountains had been hollowed, the hills terraformed and the plains raised to house immense data centers and server-farms belonging to companies like TENCENT, JD.COM, PINDUODUO and HUAWEI. Buildings covered with vegetation, inside and out, act as urban farms and look like mountains sprouting out of nowhere after an incredible tectonic movement of macro-financial investments; along the flanks of the mountains that have been peeled like fruit, forests of skyscrapers are connected by aerial corridors hundreds of meters above the ground. These suspended connections are used by swarms of couriers, drones, self-driving cars, scooters and an infinite variety of micro 3D-printed vehicles.

Shi hardly has the time to collect her backpack from the bus's luggage compartment before the rickshaw she has just booked for the last leg of her journey pulls over beside her playing the RICKALISHOW jingle.

"Hi, it's hot today, isn't it? Where shall I take you?"

The canopy, covered with solar paint, of the bamboo fiber vehicle is incandescent, but the driver, a young athletic man with an orange mohawk, turns on the air conditioning.

"Langdezhen."

The southern outskirts of Kaili are dominated by the APSARAS data center, a honeycomb structure visited by hundreds of drones shuttling between the domestic manufacturers and craft workshops scattered over the surrounding area. The entrance is guarded by two towering cloud goddess statues, from whose sixteen hands flash ideograms and letters representing the company's philosophy.

IN THE CODE / LINE AFTER LINE / WE LAY THE FOUNDA-TIONS / OF ETERNITY

LIKE SAND / GRAIN AFTER GRAIN / CALMS THE FURY OF THE SEA[29]

In fact, agribusiness is beginning to look like a dragon, with company conglomerates as the head and a myriad of Fab Labs and vege-centers as the paws.

"Are you going home because of the regeneration?" He asks her, noticing Shi's lost look.

"No, my father isn't very well, and I've come to see him. I live in Italy. Everything has changed since last time I was here."

"Uh, yeah, that's China. They have convinced farmers to be businessmen. Their children and grandchildren are coming back en masse from abroad. With blockchain and electronic payments they can do business all over the world, taking advantage of Big Data and AI, from their own homes."

------

29 From "Blockchain Chicken Farm" by Xiaowei Wang, FSGO x Logic, 2020, pag. 82.

"But the aim is to alleviate poverty and redistribute wealth in the less developed areas . . ."

"Yes, in theory," he says sceptically. "Of course, with the money received, some people have started their own business, others have become digital artisans and most people just carry on farming chickens and pigs, but in a technological way."

Yes, looking at the cultivated fields she can see the swarms of drones flying over the land, sowing seeds, watering, spraying, weeding and dealing with the duties that had for thousands of years been carried out by the farmers. Where they had once been doubled over with fatigue, they can now pilot the equipment remotely, sitting in the comfort of their favorite armchair, or else those who are better off can hire someone else to do even this for them.

Within the space of half an hour the scene changes, the road gets narrower and becomes an asphalt snake following the river, twisting and turning through the mountains. The houses thin out and have fewer and fewer stories, often wedged into nooks and crannies, and cement gives way to wood or more frequently economic composite material. The ground floors are home to shops selling basic staple goods and nutraceutical stores. Washing hangs from first and second floor windows: clothes, batik-style colorful tablecloths and roughly printed underwear. The roofs, on the other hand, are sloped, the shape that Shi remembers from her childhood.

A series of snapshots of life with her parents run through her mind: an electric bicycle in China, a skateboard in Italy. Chopsticks and forks. Green tea and espresso coffee. 3D printers, history of art, textbooks with Chinese/Italian characters and conferences about interpreting.

In that moment, her translation app notifies her of a request: a businessman in Shanghai is negotiating a deal concerning hundreds of bottles of MORELLINO DI SCANSANO red wine and needs help. Shi accepts the job and launches the virtual assistant. Her job is to check the translation made by the AI she has trained over the years. She doesn't usually have to intervene.

As soon as she reaches the bridge over the Langde, rebuilt to look just like the one washed away by a summer flood, she knows she has arrived. She waves at the carved monkeys on top of the bridge's columns and looks over the balustrade printed with scenes of rural life.

The black tiled roofs of the village appear as if in a dream: an expanse of glimmering fish scale-like roofs climbing up the hill with its terraces bordered with bamboo and banana trees; in the background the Wuliu mountains are shrouded in mist and cotton-wool balls of cloud. Langdezhen is just as she remembers it, a black pearl surrounded by vegetation.

The rickshaw stops at the bottom of the lane that leads to her house. Shi pays the fare and doesn't hang around to see what has changed. Her father is waiting for her.

As she hurries up the hill, her rolling suitcase follows her on four agile little legs. After a couple of bends, she passes the two story elementary school. She can hear some kids singing and others shouting, and then she sees the slender Jie in the doorway, the little garden with pepper plants to one side. She is wearing a floral print dress cinched at the waist with a brown band. Her eyes are clear and transparent, somewhere between green and yellow.

"Welcome back, Shi! It's been a long time, come in. He's been asking after you every hour."

Off with her sunglasses, jacket and shoes. Shi crosses the entrance and goes into the bedroom to stand by Ming's bed.

"You're here! It is so good to see you," he says, so full of emotion that he can't hold back the tears. He squeezes his eyes shut to hold the image, unwilling to let that moment go. Their long embrace is one of relief. Shi had feared he wouldn't last long enough for her to see him again, like with her mother a few years earlier.

Next to Ming, to one side, is his pupil, Yun, who nods to Shi in greeting as she prepares a welcome tea.

Shi is overcome by a vortex of emotions: she and her father haven't seen each other in this house for four years. It is her second home, a symbol of her second life and culture, but one that she has never thought of as second best.

The windows are open and the breeze coming in smells of rice straw and non-tanned leather, odors she hasn't smelled in a long time, perfumes that belong to a parallel life.

"How are you?"

He removes his oxygen mask and takes her hands in his, "Now I can feel so much more energy flowing towards me."

"Dad, I'm being serious."

"So am I. Man follows the laws of the land, the land that of Tao and the Tao that of nature," he says, almost reciting, "we mustn't shake or force the course of things."

"When you say it, it comes as a bit of a paradox."

"I have simply given nature a hand . . . even infinitely small things count."

"And are those things helping you?"

"They have done a lot. I have been living in symbiosis with nanosomes for years, but they can't do miracles. I have reached the age of eighty-eight with hardly any illnesses."

Shi turns to Yun as if asking for confirmation that her father isn't just putting a good face on things.

"Can I trust him?" She asks jokingly.

"Oh yes, it isn't the nature of things that scares the maestro, maybe the nature of man does though."

"What do you mean?"

Just then they hear a commotion at the entrance.

"Yes, yes, I know, but this is important," says a low, hoarse voice.

"Wait, wait, his daughter has only just got here," Jie replies.

An elegantly dressed man of about seventy appears in the doorway. He is wearing augmented reality glasses and leaning on an inlaid walking stick with its own display on the knob. In the other hand he is holding a classic briefcase.

"Maestro! You look well today. Shi has come to visit you from Italy, how wonderful." Then he introduces himself. "I am Bo Guo, I have been a great admirer of Maestro Cheng Ming since our days at Chongqing university."

Her father squeezes his eyes shut again, but this time he looks like it is in the hope that this apparition will vanish as soon as he opens them again.

"I have come to talk business," the man goes on, unaware of the embarrassment he is causing. He pulls a decorated box containing a bottle of MOUTAI out of his briefcase and places it on the table in front of him. Jie leans towards him, almost as if she wants to grab him by the sleeve. Yun sips her tea without offering any to the man or asking him to sit down.

"I have just come from Beijing and will be in Guizhou for a few days. If you have time, young lady, may I invite you to see our company? It isn't far, Leishan, a few kilometers to the south."

Ming opens his eyes again only to roll them. "I have already told you what I think about your company. Now I would like to spend some time with my daughter, if you don't mind."

"Of course, I apologize," says Bo Guo taking a step backwards. "Here, let me leave you my details in case you pass through Leishan," he shows them a QR code on his phone. Beneath it is a logo representing a cybernetic chicken and the word

BLOCKCH(AI)CKEN.

Shi doesn't know how to react to his outstretched arm, not least because Bo Guo hasn't moved; he is waiting, impassively, so in the end she takes the phone and scans the code.

Happy, Bo Guo makes his retreat as if he has won a battle.

"Insufferable. He has been coming here for four days without being invited," says Ming, irritated.

WEI'S SONG

Jie's room is spartan, the only furniture is an old wooden wardrobe from Grandpa Wei and a bed composed of cellulose resin on which a bamboo mat is lying. The walls are decorated with Jie's framed drawings: bright, colorful phoenixes and dragons flying across the sky and above snow-topped mountains.

As soon as Shi lies on the bed, she notices a myriad of black dots on the ceiling, ready to drop down on her. The mosquito net that used to be there has gone. Just then, Jie appears in the doorway.

"Ah, I didn't tell you because they don't bother me. You can use this," she says, flipping a switch next to the light. The ceiling lamp that looks like some kind of flying saucer starts to move across the ceiling, sucking in the insects one by one.

"But where will you sleep? I didn't want to kick you out . . . We could both fit."

"Don't worry, this used to be your room. I will sleep on the armchair in the dining room. I have a lot of little things to get done."

"*Little things* . . . you like that expression."

"It is the maestro, or rather, his philosophy."

Jie takes her leave and Shi goes to open the wardrobe to tidy away her "little things": a pair of trousers, three t-shirts, a jacket and her underwear. The shelves are occupied by four columns of piled up cassettes, and in the drawers, there are some very old magnetic tape reels. Curious, Shi starts reading the labels written in a handwriting she doesn't recognizes. She is sure it is her father's.

QINGYAN, XIDI, BASHA, ZHAOXING, HUANGGUOSHU, XIJING, FANJING

She takes one and goes back to Ming's room. Yun has just put a fresh jug of water on the bedside table and is about to leave. She has a rented a room at the end of the street.

"Dad, the wardrobe is full of cassettes and reels. Whose are they?"

"Oh, you've found them then," he says. "I wanted to talk to you about that, sit down."

She settles on the bed as Yun says goodbye and leaves.

"Grandpa Wei was a farmer, but in his spare time he played the *huqin*."

"I know, you've told me about it hundreds of times . . . how he met Grandma Hui at a New Year's party, he was playing and she was singing."

"Yes, that's true, but there's something I didn't tell you, not long before dying Grandpa made me promise to carry on with his collection."

"What collection? Of tapes?"

"Well, the cassettes contain traditional Guizhou songs that are vanishing because they are handed down orally from generation to generation. No one sings them anymore, and the ones you hear at festivals or in karaoke bars are poor, mangled copies there to create an atmosphere for the tourists. They are just sounds, without stories, whereas the original songs recorded in the villages held true treasures, wells of lost knowledge, culture and traditions swept away by modernity."

"But we can't listen to them any more . . ."

Ming breathes with difficulty in his oxygen mask. His eyelids start to droop.

"When I was small, Grandpa used to take me with him when he played to raise a little money. It was a very difficult period; we were often hungry. He would transcribe the songs and put the papers in bamboo canes. Then I got into Chongqing University and . . . those are the cassettes that are left. There should be a tape recorder or reel-to-reel device somewhere about. Ask Jie, she knows exactly where everything is in this house."

"Great, I would love to hear them."

Ming shifts closer to his daughter. "Shi, I didn't keep my promise."

There is regret in his clouded eyes.

"What do you mean?"

"After doing engineering, I started working immediately. A few years in the north and then, with your mother, we moved to Italy. When I came back, I didn't have the strength to go around with Jie to record more songs."

"Couldn't you have sent her on her own?"

"Yes, perhaps I could have done, but you know what people are like . . . Jie looks so human and young, but people in the villages are still diffident, no one would have opened up to her. The songs are intimate experiences, private, and often recount marvelous things, but also terrible and unpleasant ones."

"Would you like me to go with her?"

Ming's face opens up in a smile. "Yes, that would make me very happy, and Grandpa would be proud. There was that song . . . do you remember? I used to sing it to you when you were small."

"The birds in a cage?"

"Yes," he says, hunting through his memory. He lets his

eyes fall half-closed as he concentrates, clears his throat and whispers out a song.

The caged birds would like to glide with passion over the wooded hills,
Fish in a puddle would like to swim in running streams,
Fenced-in pigs would like to run about in green fields . . .

Then he stops, and frowns, sadly. "I've forgotten the rest . . . how does it go on?"

"Sleep now, Dad. Tomorrow we can get Jie to help us."

FARMAGEDDON

A group of young girls whizz past on scooters, skateboards, and electric bicycles.

On the right, a number of old shops have been modernized with augmented reality windows: a pharmacy, half Oriental, half Western, advertizing 160-finger massages and 160-acupuncture treatments applied by a 16-arm KUKA device, a digital artisan who accepts 3D formulas to make in real time on four parallel printers. A little further on, the tea house HARMONIOUS FRAGRANCE offers synaesthesia experiences produced by the union of taste, smell and musical mixtures.

First thing in the morning, Shi and Jie had left to go shopping. Yun had stayed behind in the garden to look after the vegetable patch where she is growing Sichuan pepper plants.

"Therefore, we don't need any of those old devices to listen to the songs?"

"No, I memorized them all years ago, when the maestro asked me to. He must have forgotten, it's his age."

"I would love to listen to them later, if you don't mind."

"Of course, when we have afternoon tea."

They go past a little lake where a water buffalo is splashing about in the middle of a carpet of lotus flowers. Shi stops to look at the fish; some of them are strangely luminescent.

"They are Carp-CRISPR," says Jie, "engineered for nocturnal illumination."

"Oh, the poor fish."

Jie frowns. "Are you sure you want to come to the market?"

"Why?"

"I wouldn't like you to get upset."

"Now you are frightening me. Is it really so bad?"

At the entrance to the market there is a five-meter-high installation: a holodrama showing the "dangers" of bad body odor. A collection of characters act out various situations: two female friends wrinkle their noses at the arrival of a "stinky" male friend, a wife kicks her husband out of their house, throwing soap and deodorants at him as he goes, a young lady with sweaty armpits is turned down at a job interview. BROMHIDROSIS (THE STINK OF THE IMMORTALS) IS AN UNPLEASANT AFFLICTION. OUR 98% EFFECTIVE NANOTECH THERAPY REMOVES ALL BACTERIA. GUARANTEE YOURSELF A PLEASANT AND HAPPY FUTURE! ONE NANITE BATH AND SAY GOODBYE TO YOUR STINK FOR EVER! People are eating and chatting noisily on the streets amongst the stalls, their arm gestures are expansive, their laughter uninhibited, just like in Italy. Nevertheless, this sense of familiarity vanishes when she sees the electrified enclosures where big screens composed of dozens of monitors have been mounted. Each enclosure is monitored by drones hovering above them.

The images show live footage of the chickens, pigs, rabbits and calves. Each animal has a bracelet around one of its legs tracking steps and movement, like those wrist devices that stimulate people to exercise through rewards and progression through levels. Except, this gadget sends data to a remote-control center analyzing the health/hygiene status of the animals. Every time the average daily step count drops below a certain pre-established level, a small electric shock forces them to move. If you watched the animals non-stop for more than five minutes, you would see their shivers and spasms.

At a certain point Bo Guo appears on the monitors, arguing with a farmer. Hearing his voice, Shi realizes that the real thing is going on just around the corner.

"Well? They've got used to it. You're running the risk of not reaching your objectives, Feng! Instead of monitoring the livestock I should be pointing the drones at you!"

Feng lowers his gaze; he is holding an ankle bracelet in one hand and a chicken's leg in the other.

"I have told you, you must never, ever, remove an ankle bracelet. The customers want to be able to read the label and follow the animal's full history. Why else do we have a webpage with the date of birth, step count, food eaten and the photos of every animal?"

"It was ill, it was pecking at its own leg."

"Then you should have called the withdrawal service. You did the course, didn't you? In case of illness or accident BLOCKCH(AI)CKEN personnel should be called, they will come equipped with gloves and masks and sort everything out."

Jie puts her arm around Shi and leads her away from the enclosures.

"Until seven years ago, Mr. Feng used to bring his chickens to us."

"I remember," she said, "they used to scratch around behind the school yard. I used to play with them when I was a kid."

"Exactly, but those were vegetarian chickens. Now they are stuffed with genetically modified soy, grain, protein powder and treated scraps to fatten them up more quickly. Quite often animal parts end up in the scraps, and the protein additives contain products of animal origin. They do this to make them meat for slaughter as quickly as possible. They become cannibals, infecting and reinfecting their own species, no wonder every now and then a pandemic breaks out. It can happen anywhere, in any battery farm, from Holland to Texas."

"What about the drones?"

"The poor chickens are neither intelligent nor brave, and if they get stuck outside their cages at night, they get scared, gather together around the light, crowding together at risk of crushing each other. Sometimes you can hear them all screaming at the same time. A kind of nightmare poultry swarm. The herding drones limit the crowding."

"Mr. Feng is no longer a farmer."

"No, the apps for facial and voice recognition, satellite images and algorithms belong to BLOCKCH(AI)CKEN, Mr. Feng has become a specialized laborer trying to fulfill as many of the online orders as possible. Every now and then he comes to Maestro Ming to get it off his chest, last year he said he got 6,000 orders for 8,000 chickens from 15 different countries."

Shi moves back to the enclosure. A chicken jerks its head suddenly. To her, it looks like it is asking for mercy.

"They aren't animals anymore, they are *animorphs*."

"Come on, let's go, the fruit and vegetable stalls are further on."

"What did Mr. Guo want the other day? What business was he talking about?"

"Ah well, he wants Maestro Ming's pepper plants, the ones Yun is caring for in the vegetable patch."

Little Big Things

There are a few rabbits hopping about in the grass under the chairs. Ming, Shi and Yun are sitting drinking tea, waiting for Jie to come into the garden. Her voice reaches them before she does, starting high she rises a number of octaves, singing a Yi language song. These sounds spread a great distance, further than the pond, even beyond the Langdezhen hill.

> *The turtle dove and chicken scratch in the dirt,*
> *The chicken has a master, the turtle dove does not,*
> *If the chicken's master comes to bring it back*
> *The turtle dove is left there all alone.*

Jie is so beautiful she is blinding, and her voice is bewitching even when she is singing about chickens and doves. Ming stands and applauds her. "Bravo, I had forgotten you memorized the songs! How lucky." Then his mood darkens, he droops, and sits back down. "So many memories."

"Dad," Shi says, in an attempt to cheer him up, "tomorrow Jie and I are going to look for more songs. Doesn't that make you happy?"

"Oh yes, I am very grateful." He sips his tea and appears to drop off to sleep. Shi's presence has reinvigorated him, he even asked to come outside to get some fresh air.

"Dad," she continues, stroking his face. "The other day Mr. Bo mentioned business. What was he talking about?"

"Oh," says Ming, hesitating. "That old fox, he's been pestering me for forty years. He wouldn't give up then, and he won't give up now!"

"Why? What happened?"

"Do you remember the nanoscope?"

"Of course, where you showed me the nanosome experiments."

"After university, I worked in an independent laboratory and our most important client was a nutraceutical company. Bo Guo was the commercial manager, he could only have been about eighteen.

"I still have the old nanoscope in the house, even though no one ever uses it anymore. At the time, it needed a monitor and a pointing interface to work, whereas now Yun can wear a pair of gloves with sensors and an augmented reality visor to manipulate and program the nanosomes on a latest generation nanomat.

"Every single week when he came to the laboratory, he would pressurize us into speeding up our deliveries of nutraceuticals. He said that the future wouldn't wait, that we had to satisfy our customers, that our prosperity depended on their happiness, all those silly things they teach in economics courses."

When she has finished her tea, Yun takes a bag and a watering can and heads towards the vegetable patch.

"He kept muttering on about his vision and tried to convince anyone and everyone of his plans. He waved his arms around, pointing at this and that, he made shapes with his hands, like boxes within boxes, growth curves, and objects flying through the air. New ideas—he would say, like someone possessed—outside-the-box innovation, business creativity."

Opening the bag, Yun starts to spread fertilizer around the stems of the pepper plants, then waters them carefully.

"He never stopped, every so often he would come along and say, 'Close your eyes, think about the future, then open them and tell me what you see.' I would open mine, hoping he had disappeared, but he never had, he was always there, in my future's way. I had a different goal. In secret, I was developing my dream of creating nanosomes that could compose vitamins, proteins and carbohydrates from raw materials like tubers, roots, leaves and bark. Simple molecules present in nature everywhere, in water, in the air, so that we wouldn't have to depend on the monster that the industrial food and farming industry had become. I had seen a future, but it was so very different to Bo's."

Yun picks a number of red berries; their color is intense and shiny, they are all split down one side where each has a seed peeking out.

"So, one day, to get him away from me, I invited him to look in the nanoscope. I was convinced he would calm down, stop pestering me, but he was struck with the conviction that he wanted to do business with me! It was a terrible mistake. Over the years Bo Guo made a name for himself, he worked for ALIBABA, he was one of the promoters of the TAOBAO villages and now despite being retired, he has begun launching start-ups with certain business angel friends of his from Beijing, like that BLOCKCH(AI)KEN you saw yesterday. Why would I be interested? I would like humanity to be able to stop eating three times a day, reducing meals to once a month. That's what nanosomes are for, to make the organism more efficient. We are already slaves to the market, there is no need to create other phenomena that increase nutritional disparity. Because that is what happens when food is treated the same way as any other commodity, to make money and speculate with. Food should be considered as a fundamental right, and if this concept sounds utopian, then we may as well make food obsolete. We may as well take food from the plates, from the fields, from the industry, from the trucks, from the planes, from the ships, from the dumps, make it vanish completely and see what happens."

Ming takes a breath. He hasn't spoken this much in months. It's as if he feels the need to hurry and tell Shi everything.

"It is a complex scenario to plan," says Jie meditatively. Her pupils shrink and thin to the shape of those of a cat as she processes these concepts.

Yun, though, comes back from the vegetable patch and places the peppercorns on the tea table.

"Just think what old Guo would give to be able to transform these little seeds into millions of server farms."

"What did you say?" Shi stutters, almost choking on her tea.

"Yes, we have been experimenting with methods of recording data on DNA," Yun continues, tasting a berry. "Maestro Ming took a sample from his nanosomes, inserted cultured stem cells and managed to integrate them in the genetic code of the pepper plants. Now they can be programmed on a nanomat. Imagine whole fields of distributed data, no longer shut inside underground data centers, but accessible to everyone and powered by the light of the sun."

Shi doesn't have clear memories of the time when her father—to follow his nanosome dream—left China, but the images of him assembling molecules at all hours of the day and night surface in her mind. When she was small, she had been able to fall asleep on a sofa like a kitten, curled up on a cushion while he split and reconnected subatomic bonds, or else, other times, she had fun chasing the molecules he had split off that flew away like clouds of steam, other times she even tried to put them together as if they were old LEGO bricks. Ming had always been an infallible maestro of nanotechnological composition and experts from all around the world would send their 3D drafts for him to analyze, correct and finalize with his patience and exceptional meticulousness. Even when she was studying at the University of Siena to become an interpreter, she saw him as a 3D design artist, somewhere between a sculptor who gave shape to objects using an infinite number of grains of rice, and those street artists who paint the flagstones with water, tenuous images that evaporated within a few hours of being created.

"Does Guo know about this?" Shi asks worriedly.

"Oh, no. Fortunately he knows nothing about it," says Ming coming suddenly awake again. "He thinks it is nutraceutical pepper, an improved version of the products enriched with nanotechnology we used to make in the laboratory. I daren't think what he might become if he discovered the true purpose of these peppercorns."

SINGING IN THE CLOUD

The entrance to the venue CELESTIAL MELODY is crowded with a queue of waiting people: groups of friends, couples and children holding their parents' hands, all quivering with the desire to listen to the storyteller.

Inside, the tables and sofas in the VIP area have been arranged in a semi-circle in front of the stage. Drinks and a hot and cold buffet arranged around the edges are available to everyone; to order, a person just has to take a photo of what they want and the amount is automatically debited.

Multicolored lasers slice through the air, smoke spreads across the room, coming from above like nocturnal mist. A baritone voice rumbles through the hall. Wearing a tunic with four wide sleeves, face painted like a theatrical mask from the Sichuan opera, the storyteller starts an ancient local legend. In a hieratic pose, he accompanies himself by drumming his fingers, tipped with little sticks, on a tambourine.

Inside an immense pumpkin used as a boat
Only two would be saved from the water
The brave Ajien and his splendid sister
Who he, without anyone else left in the world, wanted to
make his bride
She refused, it went against decorum
And proposed to roll two rocks down facing hills
If they landed on each other, he could have her as his consort

Shi rises on tiptoes to see better.

"Are you sure this is the right place?" She yells in Jie's ear.

"Yes, after the show they'll all go into the karaoke room on the floor above. If we're going to find singers anywhere, it is here."

Shi is sceptical, this show looks like a clumsy caricature of the poetic songs her grandfather used to collect for her.

In secret, brave Ajie placed two rocks, one on top of the other
And when the first ones vanished into the tall wild grass
He showed her the second two and took her with him into the
shadows.
She refused again and this time suggested they should throw
two knives
And if they landed in the same sheath then they would marry.

The audience mutters, the tension rises. Shaking bells attached to his ankles, the storyteller makes them ring as if to regain his audience's attention. Then he draws two knives from his extra sleeves and raises his voice.

Slyly Ajie hid two blades in one single sheath
And when he gathered them from the ground at the end of the
test
He took his sister to continue their story.

With a flick of his wrists, the storyteller throws the knives into a heart-shaped target. The audience cheers, applauds and begins to head towards the side stairs.

"Liar! You are a liar!" Someone shouts out. "That's not how it ends!"

Jie and Shi turn towards a young woman covered in colorful tattoos and piercings.

"Why didn't you tell the whole story, huh? What's the matter? Are you afraid of the truth?" The girl carries on venting against the storyteller.

A security man goes over to her and suggests she leaves. She resists, wriggles away from him and complains, "You're a rabbit and a coward! That song has a different ending, and you know that well, you, you *bull-teller*!" Then she is grabbed and dragged outside.

"Don't let him trick you, don't let that thing make a joke out of you!"

Shi pulls Jie behind her. The young woman's shouts recede beneath the drum rolls concluding the show.

"My grandmother knows that song."

The girl has told them that her name is Ting and she lives in Leishan. She has bronzed skin, a straight nose and slit-like eyes, and her hair is tied in bunches, like rabbit ears.

"Would you mind taking us to her?"

"Why?"

"We would like to know how the song really ends."

"My grandmother lives in the mountains. Half an hour from here."

"No problem," Jie answers, using her phone to call for a car. She pulls a face, winks, and Ting agrees.

RICE - DRONE - FISH - DUCK

Perched on the crest of a hill with BLOCKCH(AI)CKEN signs on its slopes, the land of Ting's grandmother is a strip of terraced rice paddies.

The car had left them by the side of a country road, and they were finishing the journey on foot.

"We're nearly there," says Ting, walking up a muddy path. "My grandmother, Shan, is the only person, from here to Datong, not to have sold her land."

All around them, the bleating and lowing of animals in their enclosures leads them to think intensive farming has taken over from traditional farming everywhere.

"Do you still follow the rice-fish-duck system?" Jie asks, lighting the way along the shaded footpath with her eyes.

"Yes, but she is getting old, and she can't manage on her own. Her rice fields are small and narrow, it is impossible to reach them with any kind of car. A couple of years ago I bought her three drones at Huaqiangbei Market. I had the parts sent from Shenzhen and put them together with a little help from my friends. Now Grandmother can use a hybrid rice-drone-fish-duck system," says Ting quite proudly.

The hill is steep and the rice fields are flooded, Shi notices fish in the water eating insects, they act as a natural repellent while the ducks scratching about provide the fertilizer and keep down the more voracious snails.

"Compared to her more technological neighbors, Grandmother doesn't need anything, pesticides, chemicals, additives or anti-parasitics, she carries on as she always has. Over at BLOCKCH(AI)CKEN they think farmers are only producing food for people in the cities. For them, feeding people is like feeding pigs. They don't care at all about the practices of small farmers. For thousands of years farmers have protected and maintained the land, rather than *optimizing agricultural production*."

Then she makes a gesture towards the fence coasting the footpath. She gives it a tremendous kick, alerting the surveillance drone. Its yellowish beep, beep, beep only makes her even angrier.

"Optimization, my ovaries! Surveillance capitalism! Like that bull-teller at CELESTIAL MELODY!! They are just a collection of badly written and terribly managed algorithms."

A hundred meters higher up, between a golden yellow magnolia and a moon white one, a hunched over old woman is waving at them. Above her, colored lights flashing on and off, its metallic hands opening and closing, is a drone which, upon seeing Ting, rushes towards her, gliding down from on high like a happy puppy.

"Grandmother! Is the water hot? I've brought some friends with me; they want to hear you sing!" Ting yells, running to hug her.

The drone whirls around them both and all the fuss brings another two patched-up devices fluttering from the fields, still holding bags of fruit and seeds in their hands.

Jie stops, stretches her neck like a swan, and gathers the sight of the rural beauty of this landscape shrouded with mist. Shi does the same, flaring her nostrils to breathe it all in as deeply as possible.

In the jars lining the shelves there are fish from the rice fields preserved in wine. A number of agricultural tools hang from the ceiling beams and on the walls, like museum artifacts from a far off time, rendered useless by the multi-purpose hands of the drones.

"What has happened to Zhao?" Ting asks, slapping a humandroid hard on the back. It is sitting in an unnatural pose in front of a loom.

"I don't know, he just seemed to get stuck. He even stopped talking. He's been like this since yesterday, no signs of life at all. You'll have to call one of your friends to fix him. In about a week I have to deliver the costume for the Huashang festival."

The costume is resting on the table: the fabric—smooth, bright and shiny—is made up of a single thread a millimeter thick, with incredible decorations representing dragons, geese, lions and dogs surrounded by many flowers and fruit trees. The boundaries between animal and floral species are blurred, sometimes there are animals with human heads or combinations of imaginary interspecies beings. These images are like mobile antique books of history, collections of ancient myths and legends, passed down by the oral traditions of the ancestors across hundreds of generations, motif by motif, illustrating the various ways in which the Miao see reality and energy in the soul of everything.

"It is not that simple, Grandmother. Zhao was the best embroiderer in Huaqiangbei. I'm still doing odd jobs here and there to finish paying for him."

Shan picks up some pieces of paper scattered over the ground. From the unbound pages various very fine, colored threads can be seen sticking out.

"Well," Ting's grandmother says caustically, "he can't even weave the *poxian*. You would have learned more quickly than him."

It seems that what Shan has learned over the course of her life is being passed down directly to Zhao without going through Ting.

"This again? Can you really see me threading bamboo needles for the rest of my life?! C'mon Grandmother, my friends didn't come here to watch us argue, they want to know how the story of Ajie and his sister really ends."

"All right then, you get the tea ready," Shan answers, shooing her away with a hand. As she picks up her *huqin*,

Ting pours the tea and brings out a plate of *baba*, a sticky rice treat.

Shan begins to play and sing.

. . . After nine months Ajie and his sister had a child, oh that
poor child
A deformed being, he had no legs and only stumps for arms.
His mother was in despair, and Ajie, blinded by anger
Murdered the child and cut it to pieces in shame
Then he threw the pieces far away from the hill, but when he
awoke in the morning,
He found those pieces had transformed, and were now many
men and women.
This is how the land was repopulated.

The song quiets to a tremulous note and Jie stands up to clap and thank Shan. Then she blinks her eyes twice, a sign that she has memorized the audio, and declares, "This version, recorded to the cloud, will be broadcast to whoever wants to listen to it. It will never run the risk of being forgotten again."

Hearing a buzzing sound, Shi realizes the drones have been hanging around outside the window, listening to old Shan's singing. They bob from left to right, like over-excited rust buckets, this is their way of showing their appreciation.

"My grandfather used to go around the villages collecting local folk songs," Shi says. "My father did the same until he went to Italy, now we are going to carry on the tradition."

"Your grandfather must have been Chen Wei, then. And you are the daughter of Maestro Ming."

"Yes, do you know them?"

"Of course, we had lots of parties together. I was a friend of your mother; we sewed many, many dresses when she still lived in the village . . ." Then she stops and apologizes, covering her mouth with her hand.

"Don't worry. It happened years ago," Shi reassures her.

Shan gets up as if she has suddenly remembered something. "I thought I put it here," she says, opening drawers in the kitchen dresser. "Here we are ... What a coincidence, she made this. It took her two years. She must have been a little younger than you are now."

Shan shows them a ceremonial robe made of finely embroidered cotton. Geometric floral designs descend down the sleeves to the cuffs. The collar is embroidered with triangles and swastikas, whereas on the back there is a representation of the Butterfly Mother, an ancient Miao symbol of life and transformation, flying over an undulating foam of stylized waves.

"I would like you to take it to Maestro Ming. A gift from the past, from his wife, your mother."

SHANZHAI

Shi rushes into the house carrying the robe.

"Dad, look! I have a gift for you from ..."

As she crosses the threshold of the bedroom she stops, shocked. Her father is holding the end of his stick pressed like a weapon against Mr. Feng's chest. Feng, his eyes down and head pulled in against his shoulders, is apologizing with a series of bows.

"What's going on?"

Shi is disconcerted and turns to Jie in the doorway, hunting, and failing, to find an explanation.

"Yun surprised our old friend Feng stealing from the garden," says Ming. "His pockets were full of peppercorns."

"I apologize, Maestro, I wasn't doing it for me. BLOCK-CH(AI)CKEN meat is so tasteless without spices. I've heard people say your pepper is the best in all of Sichuan."

"And where did you hear this chitchat?" Yun interrupts.

Shi calms down and places the robe on the foot of the bed, things aren't as they seem.

"From Mr. Bo Guo, he asked me to come here and sneak in to pick some pepper samples for growing, without being seen."

"Oh, yes?" Maestro Ming says, rubbing his beard. "So you're telling me Bo Guo decided to send you here to steal because he knew we would never give him our peppercorns, is that right?"

"I think so. You know, Maestro . . . I would never have come to steal from you," Feng answers, bowing even lower. "But it's difficult to make ends meet these days, the orders keep growing, but the profit margins on meat get smaller and smaller."

"You are right, I do believe you. This is not your fault."

"I would rather stop raising those poor animals like that. I can't bear to see their suffering, but what can I do?"

Yun throws a complicit look at the maestro who, in turn, sighs and pulls his stick away from Feng.

"*Shanzhai,*" he says solemnly. "Do you remember this concept of copies and imitations of Western technological products for which we were criticized and derided for years? That term referred to the 'outlaws' who fought in the mountain villages for autonomy, independence and a kind of survival. In the West, they never understood the deepest sense of the word, because *shanzhai* means incremental collective knowledge, co-opting the necessary resources, high speed sharing, reusing what works and recycling what can still be used, all in a decentralized manner, for the billion people who are at the base of the technological pyramid. And yes, it is also an alternative idea to the Western one of intellectual rights and obsessive copyright protection."

The maestro coughs, it seems like he wants to get a lot of things off his chest in this conversation. "The West has stopped innovating," he continues, tossing a few of the peppercorns up and down in his hand. "They are only really concerned with slowing down their own technological development and blocking that of others in order to maintain a competitive advantage with which they can enjoy the well-being they have gained to the disadvantage of the rest of the world. Please, Yun, show him what we mean . . ."

Yun puts on the visor and switches on the holograph. The compositional diagram of a nanite fluctuates in the air. After a moment, she begins to manipulate the view and says, "The maestro is right. Today at Huaqiangbei Market, where modern *shanzhai* was born, you can buy 3D printed organs, satellite microphones with integrated speakers, 100TB playlists and solar-powered modular phones. Intellectual rights aren't an intrinsic value, just like legal ownership and private property. It's an old English idea from the 1800s that belongs to the obscurantist vision of the world in which competition was considered more important than cooperation. How can anyone innovate if they can't afford the tools necessary to do so?"

Zooming in on the view, Yun shows the various components of the miniscule miracle, similar to a stem cell capable of differentiating itself into other more specific ones. Two motors and a gyroscope allow the nanite to move, a calibration system with a manipulator makes it possible for it to grab subatomic particles and a cellular membrane-type sensor allows it to recognize the nature of the world around it.

"Like a collective work of art, created thanks to the efforts of many artists, the engines of creation are the fruit of the work of the best nanosmiths in the world," says Ming. "I simply helped them put the pieces together, inside me. If the West has used military invasion weapons, cultural colonization, economic imperialism and one-way technological globalization, why can't we defend ourselves with cunning?"

Spinning slowly, the nanite displays its parts: a wireless antenna, a wavelength sensor, organized logic circuits, a T-cell anti-receptor and an emergency self-destruct system.

Suddenly Yun opens all ten fingers and the nanite instantly multiplies with an amazing effect, then she makes it smaller, leaving a cloud of a very fine dust of luminous particles fluctuating in the air. Feng watches these movements, as if hypnotized, his mouth hanging open.

"If I have the right to use something," Yun adds, "I also have the right to modify it, change it, reuse it, regenerate it and even claim it as mine. In the world that is coming, *shanzhai* applied to nanosomes could liberate humanity from a number of biological needs and become a precious tool for decolonizing technology, and therefore the future."

Maestro Ming lifts his walking stick again, but this time points it at Feng with a benevolent smile.

"You came looking for Sichuan pepper, but you ended up finding much, much more: a radical transformation for the few ready to embrace it . . . Tell me, dear Feng, are you ready?"

"Yes . . . yes, I am. Anything to get away from those enclosures of death."

"You will be able to go back to your chickens and cockerels of before, the ones that used to give us so many fresh eggs."

"Just like old times, Maestro?"

"Just like old times, but without needing to eat them."

To all of their surprise, Jie starts singing. Her voice makes Yun's holograph vibrate, as if the two realities can communicate, interact and unite with each other.

The turtle dove would like to glide with passion over the wooded hills,

Fish in a puddle would like to swim in running streams,
Fenced-in pigs would like to run about in green fields . . .
So I claim the air, the water and the earth of the southern
fields
To give back the harvests of the lands to their inhabitants.

"Yes! That's how the song I used to sing to you when you were small ends!" Says Ming, turning to Shi and clapping for Jie. "That song was my inspiration to give nanosomes the vital breath that pervades everything, from subatomic particles to black holes. It doesn't matter how, or how long we will take, one meal at a time, we will be able to save people, animals, the whole world. Now it is Feng's turn."

Shi takes the ceremonial robe from the bed and hands it to her father.

"Mum would be happy. This is from Shan, from the village of Leishan."

Ming brushes the fabric with his fingers, sniffs at the cotton and strokes the decorations as if he is communicating with his wife. His eyes fill with tears, his lips quiver. In the same moment, Shi takes his rough, wise hand.

"Please, sing again, Jie," Shi asks her friend.

Perhaps the reason for life doesn't lie in looking for meaning, but in the possibility of reinventing ourselves an infinite number of times.

"There it is! Down there! Land!" Billai yelled, nearly falling off the dinghy.

We all looked in the direction she indicated with her arm. The waves that had shaken us for some hundred hours didn't jolt us as much as her words.

We couldn't feel our legs or move a muscle. Tangled one on top of the other, we were groggy from hunger and thirst. Muna, seated next to me, hugged her baby closer. The three guys in front exchanged a hopeful smile. Meanwhile, Haziz—who came to Bengasi after crossing the Bamako Desert—shook his hand.

"It can't be Italy. We're still far."

We looked at each other anxiously. Someone had fainted. To revive him, we had to slap his face. It wasn't a boat that we had navigated in, but a coffin.

"He's right," said Professor Kysmayo, the ex-radio host from Nairobi. "The outline is too simple. It's not the coast . . ."

Nobody said anything else, because nobody dared pronounce the name that, for some weeks, was circulating the Mediterranean's southern shores.

A dark and continuous line occupied the horizon from Otranto in Italy, arriving in Orikum in Albania. Smooth and unassailable, the bulkheads of the naval blockade rose for thirty meters on the sea waves; assembled easily thanks to the ships' containers full of carbon, but impossible to climb or break down, they represented a momentary solution (even though there were those who would've called it the "definitive deterrent") to immigration towards Europe by the sea.

"They said this part was free!" Billai shouted.

"They lied," Haziz said, almost in a whisper.

"Maybe not . . . I heard that barriers can be 3D printed overnight. The same bulkheads could've been between Pantelleria, Lampedusa and Malta . . . to force boats to turn around or follow long and expensive routes," Professor Kysmayo said.

Billai rubbed her temples with her fingers. Every border depressed her, and getting closer to a wall, erected for the sole purpose of separating international and domestic waters, discouraged her even further. With her life savings, she had crossed with me the borders of Kenya, Sudan and Libya before attempting the Benghazi crossing.

"Why didn't they tell us?" Muna said.

Nobody felt like answering such a naive question.

"They want to canalize boats to navigable checkpoints," the professor said. "And then come those . . ." he concluded, pointing to a spot in the distance.

Some black spots, which from far away looked like seagulls, revealed themselves to be surveillance drones activated by the boat's movement detected by satellite. I'd heard about those, and others used in the mountains to secure Europe's land borders. Soon, they circled over us like vultures.

With a solemn air, as if she were about to declare war on the world, Billai rose to her feet. Swaying, she grasped my back so as not to fall and said, "We've all lived through things that we shouldn't have lived through and would be better to forget. I'm not turning back. Those drones are informing someone. They'll come and take us. Doctors Without Borders, NGOs, the Coast Guard . . ."

Four hours later, one hundred and thirty-two of us were saved.

I was seventeen years old, and my life was contained in a backpack: a bar of soap, a smartphone and charger, a sports jersey (number ten, Ike Kamau) and a photo of my mom and brother. They always told me that I had a narrow head, pointed chin and quick eyes, black like tar. Like my dad's.

I was seventeen years old, and my life had been spent in a refugee camp; since when we had arrived in Dadaab from Nairobi, I hadn't seen anything but tents, dust, fences and gates.

Soft clouds glided over the sea: that night the stars would disappear, and the moon would have illuminated us all if another silhouette hadn't appeared to divert the way of our gazes and our lives.

"That's an . . . aircraft carrier?" Billai asked.

An immense structure stood out on the dark waters.

"I don't know," I said while she drew near me. The lapping of the water had worn down her combative temperament.

Someone took a picture, but in the high seas there wasn't a strong enough signal to transform anxiety into hope. It could have been a military ship charged with bringing us back to the dark side of the Mediterranean, but instead the man who drew near us on a lifeboat with four sailors told us a different story.

"Welcome," he said in English. He had blond hair tied back in a ponytail, a pronounced nose and lips and a smile, sincere but strained. "My name is Sergio Torriani and that's a Green Ship," he added, pointing behind him. "We take in anybody who needs help."

The sailors threw us water bottles.

Haziz grabbed my sleeve and asked me to translate. I was one of the few on board, along with Professor Kysmayo, who knew some English besides Swahili. When I was little, I listened to his show "Indie Reggae, Beats & Rock" on Radio Kenyamoja.com, and I knew hundreds of songs by heart.

"We don't want to board. We want Europe," I said dryly, gesturing to Haziz to show Sergio who those words came from.

He didn't answer right away, but instead tossed us a line that Billai caught in the air. "Europe doesn't want you," he continued, bitter, "and they don't care if you're escaping from hunger or war, if you live in refugee camps or if your children and grandchildren will be born and grow up in those prisons. Where do you come from?"

I heard the names of camps I knew, like Dadaab, Nyarugusu and Bokolmanyo, and others I ignored like Urfa, Zaatri and Adiharush.

"Besides, this isn't a boat for transit," Sergio said.

"So, you'll bring us back or send us to a center for identification and deportation." I translated for Muna, who'd lifted the bundle with her son inside.

"No deportation. The Green Ship is a humanitarian project for the rescue of political refugees and climate migrants."

"If you're not bringing us back and you're not going to Europe, where are you going?" Professor Kysmayo asked. He was the only one to reason with his head and not his heart.

Sergio and the other sailors were already throwing lines to ease the transfer onto their lifeboat.

"Board and you'll see."

Once we'd boarded, Sergio asked, "Nobody else?"

We looked at each other without the courage to respond. Then Professor Kysmayo said, "In the hold there were two cadavers. They died two days ago. They started to stink. We had to leave them at sea . . . to lighten our load."

"Their names?"

We were silent. Sergio added two Xs to the list of one hundred twenty-three.

From the parapet, I observed the wake of boats in transit in the Aegean Sea: a Greek ferry, two cargo boats, a cruise ship. Who knew how many immigrants were hidden like cargo in the holds.

The others were still sleeping among the trees, and they were not alone: hundreds of strangers were camping in sleeping bags and tents, and below, thousands were squished in the bunks. Yesterday evening, I didn't see anything because I quickly lay down to rest, but now, by the light of dawn, things appeared more clearly.

"Jambo," Sergio said in Swahili, offering me a cup of coffee.

"Jambo, and thank you for picking us up," I said, taking a sip.

"Did you sleep? It's not easy after being on a dinghy."

He must have had experience with migrants to speak like that.

"Little and poorly."

"Later we'll have a soccer game with everyone. Would you want to join?"

I nodded a yes and he convinced me to tell him about "our" games in Nairobi.

"Two things were important for me: surviving and playing soccer . . . then it became only one when men from al-Shabaab came to the fields where my brother Noor and I played. They scolded us because we wore shorts and played with a ball. Soccer was a decadent pastime for them . . . like alcohol, cigarettes or film. But Noor and I played it just the same, hidden. Our games ended when the bombs dropped."

I took the Ike Kamau jersey from my backpack.

"Here you can play without anyone saying anything to you."

I gave him the empty coffee cup. "This ship is really odd."

It was his turn to tell me something.

"According to international law, it's not a ship, but a micronation. First it was a bioconservation project funded by the United Nations, a bit like the seed deposits in the Norwegian Svalbaard Islands. Ever heard of it?"

I shook my head.

"Then it was converted to manage the immigrant crisis in the Mediterranean."

Three hills, in the middle of which ran a stream, recreated microclimates: temperate, desert and Mediterranean. My gaze wandered to the Mediterranean habitat where tens of drones hurried around like birds that watered leaves, cut branches, checked flowers and collected pollen, while some gardeners oversaw the operations to maintain everything green. Then, in the middle of the eucalyptus grove, I saw an impressive sequoia, its fronds shading half of the ship.

"The habitats," Sergio continued, "are protected by geodetic cupolas one hundred fifty meters tall. Fresh water comes from a desalinator powered by solar energy."

In the meantime, Billai had woken up and joined us.

"How did you manage to create . . . all of this?" she asked as if she'd woken into a dream. While I translated, Sergio showed us along a path.

Professor Kysmayo noticed us and joined up. His background as a radio journalist got the better of his sleepiness. When he wasn't on the air with "Indie Reggae, Beats and Rock," he edited a feature on technology.

"We bought an abandoned aircraft carrier, and we modified it through a crowdfunding project. The hull belonged to *Variago*, an aircraft carrier in the same class as Admiral

Kutnetzov launched in 1988 in Russia. In 2004 it was re-baptized *Liaoning* and sold to China to become a floating theme park, like Disneyland, but luckily it didn't happen. We bought it for a token price to make a botanical garden. Ours is a scientific project approved by the United Nations, though now we're more public transit for migrants," Sergio said with a laugh.

The ship flew its own flag: a sequoia styled green on a hull over a white background.

"We can host seven thousand people. We grow crops and raise livestock. We have internet and 3D printers for any needs."

"Do you want to bring all refugees aboard?" I asked, jokingly. "Like Noah's ark?"

"Impossible. You'd need a hundred ships," Billai added, "and only to evacuate the camp in Dadaab."

"In fact, we have another plan. When the time is right, we'll head towards India and the southern seas."

"Somebody won't like that solution," Kysmayo said.

Haziz and some other guys had boarded reluctantly. They'd continued to complain about wanting only Europe.

"Once they feel better, they have to decide whether or not to retry their journey. We had to save them and let them know the risks."

Streaks of lightning invaded the northern sky. From the Indian hinterlands the cloudy front advanced slowly, like a wounded animal with its head swaying. The weather warped ahead, rumbling and hiding every ray of sun. Lights descended on the water after flashing along incandescent segments.

Many of us retreated to the tents to safely enjoy this spectacle of light, water and wind while others ran through the torrential rain to refresh themselves in song and laughter.

Muna played with her son, alive thanks to the fact that he'd never been removed from his mother's breast, from which he managed to suck every drop of milk she managed to produce without dying from dehydration.

But the celebrations were interrupted when a man came down from the bridge with a megaphone in hand.

"Attention! Attention! They've detected a seaquake. Time of impact is four minutes."

A sinister light whitened the sea. Billai curled into me.

"It'll never end...even the sea has it in for us."

"Would you have preferred to do as Haziz and his friends did?"

"No, they're crazy to return to Somalia and retry that hopeless journey. But what end will we meet?"

"They say they wanted to retry, but their eyes said otherwise. We'll meet a better end. I'm sure of it."

In the middle of rolling waves four meters tall that battled the ship's hull, another one appeared: it occupied all of the horizon, and judging by the distance, it must've been three times as high. Visibility lowered and a wall of water, misty with the gusts of wind, rustled the branches of the floating forest.

The pitch, already agitated every time the ship sank into the gulch of the waves, became insupportable. Songs and screams became complaints and curses. Those who danced before now grasped onto something, trying not to vomit.

The clamor escalated, an uproar of wind, pounding of water, a vibration like a drumroll beating the charge. Despite the five-hundred-meter length and its scary tonnage, even the Green Ship suffered from the force of nature.

When the tsunami washed over us, into every pore, nerve and muscle of our bodies, Billai, her lips trembling with fear and emotion, kissed me on the lips.

Once the storm ended, lights appeared on the horizon.

When we were closer, I made out numerous boats linked together by a series of ropes and jetties: together they all formed a type of flotilla.

None of us had any idea where we'd arrived, even though that assembly in the high sea didn't seem to be our final destination. To find an answer, I went to Sergio, who was on the phone.

"Where and when did it happen?" He was asking someone. A contagious joy appeared on his face, as if he just discovered that he'd become a father.

"And how big is it?"

He walked back and forth, unable to contain his mysterious happiness.

"Yes, definitely . . . send me a scan and the coordinates. I'll inform the flotilla."

Once he hung up, Sergio grabbed me by the shoulders.

"We've been blessed. Nature is building your new home."

"A new home?"

"The seaquake . . . it opened a fault line under the ocean from which magma is pumping out."

"Are you bringing us into a volcano?"

"No, but as soon as the magma cools, we can claim the island that's emerging from the sea. Now we too have something to teach Nature. Then with the flotilla we'll think of the rest."

"The rest? That's just going to be a rock."

"Yes, at first it'll be uninhabitable, but we'll terraform it."

I turned my gaze from Sergio's satisfied face to the geodetic cupolas. Tree pollen and mushroom spores floated around, carried by the ocean breeze.

The Green Ship took the lead of the flotilla. Seen from above, it might look like a school of fish migrating for the season. And we were part of that flow.

The sign posted on top of our new land had been modified. By changing an N into a D, it was transformed from "No Man's Land" to "No-Mad Land," as the media had hastened to rebaptize the newly born micronation.

The islet where Sergio had first planted the flag—in his haste, called "No Man's Land" to underline its independence from whoever wanted to claim the territory—in time became "No-Mad Land" for us. A place accessible without a passport, entry visa or residency permit. A land designed to welcome people instead of turning them away.

I liked the wordplay of No-Man and No-Mad. Having grown up in a refugee camp between walls and gates, I'd been freed of those limits, and I'd left all borders behind. Because borders, political or mental, are temporary obstacles. Because only those who have been turned away or who have enough imagination and empathy for others know how to appreciate the value of hospitality.

The accidental but highly probable birth of the islet in the middle of the Indian Ocean was followed by a phase of movement of thousands of tons of sand from the adjacent seafloor. Thanks to pumping systems, the aspirated sand provided construction material for five enormous 3D printers.

Two of them, aboard tankers, employed the same techniques that the Dutch used to tear the polders from the North Sea—creating dikes of natural material—to protect the central atoll. Yet, different from the polder, the architects supporting the project had thought up a porous, artificial structure that, adequate to host marine life, over the course of centuries would in part replace the irremediably damaged Great Barrier Reef.

The other printers focused on terraforming the cooling magma, rich with fertile substances. They mixed it with sand from the seafloor.

It took us six months before we could set foot on "No-Mad Land."

To our touch, the ground was not hard, but instead it seemed fat and ready to be cultivated.

Under an orange sky, a carpet of yellow narcissus welcomed Billai and me. The air smelled fresh, and the land emanated a narcotic warmth, stronger than the *chillum* that Noor smoked at the camp in Dadaab. The corollas of the flowers reached Billai's bare knees, and I filled myself with the smell of the narcissus, transplanted to the island from the Green Ship months ago.

"Do you know why I like it here?" she asked as she lay down.

I shook my head.

"Because we're all immigrants from somewhere."

"If you think about it, Dadaab was also like that."

"But it's prettier here," she said, her smile showing disappointment.

I stared at her frail ankles. The first time I saw her at the refugee camp, she and two other girls were chatting while pumping water from a well. Each filled three jugs, two to carry by hand and one to balance atop their heads. They were three queens, models who strutted on dirt roads as if they were high fashion runways. She wore a long, colored skirt, a scarf on her head, earrings, coordinated makeup, hair in tiny, neat braids. Her balanced gait was perfect, her gaze ahead, noble, full of nonchalance. She shone with her own light, a star with black skin that emanated a supernatural aura as she passed, wiggling her hips between trash barrels, plastic waste, mismatched shoes, rusted pipes and goats that grazed on what they could find.

We made the whole trip together. Sometimes, like in Sudan, I feared that she wouldn't be able to make it, like when we had to bribe the guy at the border. Or when she was hurt while we were crossing an area mine-laden by Boko Haram terrorists. But more than anything else, I feared for her life the night when two traffickers cornered her after realizing her beauty. She tried to defend herself, to stop the violence. She shouted for help, crying "Saidia! Saidia!" but nobody moved for fear of being thrown in the sea for defending her. In the end, I couldn't stand it. I grabbed one of them by the neck and I flung him off the boat. The other kicked my back, grabbed my shirt and lifted me off the ground. I too would've ended up in the water had it not been for Professor Kysmayo, whose strong hands freed me from the grip of the trafficker and then threw him too into the dark waters.

"You're right, Billai . . . but unlike Dadaab, besides us all being immigrants, there's something else that makes me love this place."

"What?"

"That here, if we want, we can emigrate."

She took my hands and said in her solemn tone, "How it has always been and always will be."

Once in a while, I talked with people back in Dadaab on the Internet. Nobody wanted to admit that the refugee camp—provisional since the ninetiess—had become a permanent establishment. Not the local functionaries who received funding to continue operation, not the United Nations that paid to not solve the problem, not the refugees, forced to live there without hope of leaving. I would never want to return there to survive, imagining a life elsewhere. My elsewhere, like that of many others, was being born from the commitment of all who participated in "No-Mad Land." If we'd created a precedent better than Sealand, the Republic of Minerva and Rose Island, to cite some cases Sergio had talked about, who knew what we'd be able to achieve? Who knew if international law would adapt to the fundamental necessities of humans?

My mother and brother were already on their way to intercept the path of the Green Ship.Professor Kysmayo climbed down to the islet and waved to greet us. In his other hand he held an envelope with a round object inside.

"Down there, did you see it?"

We stood up and followed him until we reached the top of another hill where there was a second meadow, green and flat.

"They taught me how to use the 3D printer."

White lines were traced into the side of the field.

"This is my first ball," he said, pulling the object out of the envelope and raising it above his head like a trophy. And then he gave the ball a kick.

A soccer goal awaited only us.

SHAMANKA ROCK

"Can you see anything?" Miriam shouts to Kenshij after tugging the rope connecting them. The snow is so thick he has to wipe it off the phone's screen to open iMaps. The wind was howling angrily through the trees at a glacial frequency.

Kenshij doesn't use words to answer. He nods, and to indicate that they are nearly there, raises his index fingers.

The Arctic air, channelled along Lena River, is driven on to the Primorskiy ridge, where it narrows as it heads towards Lake Baikal, as if in a natural wind tunnel, to finally find release with the strength of a storm.

The yellowish glow of some headlights and *isba* lights catches their attention and then vanishes. On one side there is a wall of impenetrable white, on the other side the hill plunges down to the frozen surface of the lake.

Miriam tugs at the rope again, "Shouldn't it be here?"

The signal is close. Kenshij opens his arms, around him he can only see the incessant fluttering of the falling snow. They start walking again, sinking into the icy blanket of snow. Then, missing her step, Miriam stumbles and falls into a ditch by the side of the road.

Kenshij stops suddenly like a horse who has been reined in.

"Wait! There is someone here!" Miriam yells.

He retraces his steps and helps her free the body from the lethal embrace of the snow. They get him out of the snow with difficulty and, once free, the man, half frozen, shivers, hardly able to move.

Miriam digs around in the stranger's pockets and Kenshij rubs his arms and legs energetically.

"Yes!! This is who signalled us," shouts Miriam, pulling a GLOBAL WALKER customized phone from his jacket.

From the north, the *Sarma* wind burns and blows on their faces at 100 kilometers per hour; but when the man opens his eyes a crack, he jumps, stunned.

The figures in front of him aren't wearing coats or gloves, they aren't wearing scarves around their necks or hats on their heads. Weak light is coming from their helmets, but other than this they are dressed for a Siberian summer, t-shirts and hiking shorts.

"Who are you?"

The man looks around him. His attention is on the frescoed walls of the cave painted with natural pigments representing an idyllic valley with circular yurts amongst wild horses.

"Igor . . . my name is Igor Mikhailovic Semionov."

He knew this place: for the Evenki nomadic shepherds it is the birthplace of the legendary ancestor, whereas the Buddhist monks believe a Mongolian divinity lives in the cave. This is why Shamanka Rock is a pilgrimage destination for both the Buryats and communities scattered across Mongolia, Siberia and Kazakhstan.

There are some animal skin-covered benches and the ground is scattered with votive offerings, jewels and pots made by the best digital craftspeople in the area.

The cave is a covered sanctuary.

"I am Miriam Farchi, and this is Kenshij Shimizu. It's lucky the battery didn't run out."

"It doesn't matter, you have to see the lake."

Igor looks at the woman's wrinkled hands. He can see faded, moving marks on her epidermis, like dynamic arabesques from her fingertips to her elbows and on up under her short sleeves.

"Tomorrow morning, as soon as the storm has passed."

Igor lets his eyes close some. His breathing is labored. "We have to leave here. The cave is forbidden to strangers."

"We will, but this is the only shelter. You would die of hypothermia within a few hours outside."

"You could have left me where I was; now that you are here, my job is done."

"Don't say that. What has happened?"

Behind them, Kenshij is preparing an infusion of linden and mallow. He has taken some snow and is heating it in a pan over a small fire he has made. Next to him, a nanomat has just finished printing a cellulose cup.

"It's not worth hearing about," Igor answers bitterly.

"If you called us, it means you still care about something."

"The Baikal is the only thing . . ."

Kenshij offers Igor the cup, but he refuses to drink.

"Ah, so that's how it's going to be, is it?" Says Miriam, standing now to see the cave paintings better. "You are not the first stubborn donkey I have run into . . . My son was just the same, such obstinate resignation, before the nanites."

Igor's gaze follows her movements, that word has made him curious. "Are those what make the marks under your skin? I have seen some videos."

"More or less," she says, lifting her sleeve to uncover her shoulder. An intense, greenish glow lights up the space. "But these are *heliotrons*, nanites make less of an impression."

"That's why I called you. You have to do something."

"Perhaps you could do something too, instead of feeling sorry for yourself."

Igor lowers his eyes. He can feel a huge weight of guilt lying on his shoulders. He deserves some of it, but not all.

"Is it true that the sun feeds you?"

"It's an exaggeration. Some of us get our nutrition from the fruits of the earth, some from the sun's rays, but its more complicated than that. However, every one of the PULL-DOGS has embraced some form of *ecolution*."

Kenshij offers the cup to Igor again, but he continues to avoid it.

"If you tell me what has happened to you, I will tell you about us."

"All right then," he says finally, accepting the cup. He starts to drink, but after a few sips his eyes droop and Miriam watches as he falls asleep.

At dawn Kenshij is out doing his Qi Gong exercises; Miriam goes over to Igor to ask him to carry on from where they left off last night.

"I have lived in an isolated valley near Novosibirsk for ten years. I was a builder, odd jobs here and there to begin with, and then with a firm which won a contract to compose a hospital. Unfortunately, when the building was finished, a summer fire destroyed the site and everything else within a radius of forty kilometers."

"The terrible one of 2032?"

"No, the year after. It was hardly talked about, so as not to spread panic."

"Yes, short-term short-sightedness. Did you study before that?"

"Botany, I liked growing plants. I had to work as a builder because they were only hiring ex-military pilots who could fly drones in precision agriculture. Nobody wanted to dirty their hands with earth then, and even less so now."

"But did you have a greenhouse?"

"Of course, in the family *dacia* in Irkutsk. I grew cucumbers, potatoes and tomatoes. Why all these questions?"

"Because there are *walkersways* running along the deforested corridors that used to be used for high tension pylons, others are being created along abandoned railways and others are repurposing roads fallen into disuse because of the arrival of the motorways. Along these paths, independent self-sufficient provision stations—spontaneously but logically—are popping up, places where walkers can find seasonal produce in solar greenhouses georeferenced on GLOBAL WALKER. In this way, during transhumances, fruit and vegetables can be available to everybody. The only contribution asked for in return is a few hours of work looking after the plants."

"What if someone doesn't respect the rules?"

"Well, so far that hasn't been a problem. Mutual help is a deep feeling, it takes years of exposure to the worst of competitive capitalism to eradicate it. However, if someone behaves badly it is reported and, if it continues to happen, they are expelled from the circuit, which is managed by blockchain to avoid further possible incidents. The greenhouses are monitored by video surveillance marbles and defended by stun drones."

"My dream was to grow an avocado plant, to grow an avocado pear like the one I ate in Turkey, when I was on holiday by the Black Sea, with Irina."

"Your wife?"

"She was," Igor's mood darkens again. "Stomach cancer. Late diagnosis."

Miriam attempts to probe other paths without making him clam up again.

"How did you end up here?"

"Last year, when the greenhouse was blown away by a storm, I couldn't cope any more . . . I wanted to end it all, but first I wanted to see Lake Baikal one last time, so I came to Olkhon Island and saw the disaster. It was too much. I tried to talk to people, to convince people not to leave, but nothing... I lost all hope too, bit by bit. Then I sent you the report . . . It's easy to take the road to desperation around here, it starts with a beer or two, turns into too much vodka and ends with drowning in alcohol or falling into a ditch."

"It's lucky I fell into that ditch too."

Igor doesn't react to her joke; he puts his hands in his hair thinking about all those misadventures.

"Y'know, the hospital that went up in smoke isn't the only place people can be cured and the greenhouse isn't the only place people can find food."

"What do you mean?"

"There are other methods of . . ."

In that moment, Kenshij comes back into the cavern. He is waving his arms, about to tell them that someone is coming.

"They are already here," says Igor, worried. "The drones must have seen us."

"Who? Do you know them?"

"The mayor of Khuzhir, Nikolai Šelichov and his gang of supporters. I warned you."

Miriam and Kenshij hurry to gather their things together, they heave the backpacks up onto their shoulders and leave the cave. Igor follows them, not really convinced.

SPIROGYRA

The sky has cleared, but a scattering of clouds up high and a handful of dwarf pines with contorted roots clinging to the side of the hill are not enough to pacify the panorama. The idyll is marred by a line of larches reduced to a blackened watermark and birch trees swaying like scared ghosts.

This desolation, exacerbated by the winter, only makes their progress more difficult.

Behind them, Shamanka Rock looks like a meteorite that has plunged into the frozen lake.

A hundred meters away, a procession of about thirty people led by a bearded man with a combative air flourishing a stick, more as a weapon than as a means of support, are making their way towards them. "Igor, I knew it!" Yells the bearded man, speeding up his stride. "Only you would bring outsiders to camp in our sacred cavern!"

"We apologize," Miriam intervenes, "Igor was close to dying from hypothermia and the only shelter we could find was here in the cave. It saved his life."

The people with the mayor are staring at the bare elbows and knees of Miriam and Kenshij with inquisitive eyes, their curiosity heightened by those strange tattoos. In reaction and because of the gusting *Sarma*, they pull their coats closer around them and tug their fur hats down over their ears. Nevertheless, the mayor calms down as if pleased by the idea, in front of his community, that the Shamanka Rock could have life-saving powers.

"In any case, women are forbidden to enter the shamans' cave," he adds sternly.

"We didn't mean to offend anyone. We are just leaving."

"It isn't so simple. You'll have to pay a fine."

"What?" Miriam is stunned, but she remembers all the many times—with the PULLDOGS—she had encountered these hostile attitudes: thrown off the Garbatella-Testaccio viaduct in Rome, driven away from Fosso Bianco on Mount Amiata, removed from the calanques in the Tuscan-Emilian Apennines, searched on the Green Ark in Istanbul—with every entry, a request for information; with every exit, a proof of passage; with every digression, a sanction; with every movement, a punishment or a warning. At every attempt to remove an identity from their backs, someone else always ran to stick them with another one, as if this were the only way to interact with other people.

"The cavern is not a hotel, it is our natural sanctuary," the mayor declares.

In other places, during their years of walking over Siberian Russia, Miriam had already come across this lack of consideration for strangers. This time, the ban seems to be connected to local beliefs about women being "impure sinners" who might contaminate sacred places. On the other hand, other *babushkas* had whispered to her that the ban was there to protect women, as visiting a sanctuary full of such mysterious and uncontrollable energy could cause complications during childbirth.

Far from the towns, whole communities had refused modernity, regarding it as too rational and inappropriate to their needs. They had gone back to the traditions of the old days, which were often similar to the superstitions: baptizing babies in the waters of the rivers and lakes, burying their dead in the forests, planting trees instead of gravestones. Many areas had, in this way, challenged the decadence of European Russia and the American Dream; in lawless Siberia, where politics didn't have a strong hold, more and more people were choosing to live in a kind of "no man's land" where they could feel like themselves. When she had left Rome, even Miriam, though for different reasons, felt some of this, the desire to start a new world within the old one.

"Don't be ridiculous," she says, wading into the procession. "We haven't had money for at least six years. We are here to see the Baikal, at Igor's request."

At these words, the people begin to murmur and the mayor's tone changes. "Really? Can you help us?"

"It's too early to say. We have only seen a few photos. We have to evaluate the situation in person."

On the surface of the lake, they can see cyclists, surfers and runners. Around here, in the winter, the Baikal Ice Marathon is run between the towns of Tanhoi on the eastern bank, and Listvyanka on the western bank. The race, one of the most extreme in the world, attracts hundreds of athletes from all around the world.

"They are the only source of income left to us," the mayor says, a sense of dejection showing, but also a hint of pride.

"With your permission, we would like to camp outside town. We don't want to cause any problems," Miriam says.

Kenshij and Igor follow, leaving the crowd behind them.

"Why must we always help with or witness a disaster to feel human?"

The previous evening, because of the bad visibility, they hadn't noticed the blotches along the shoreline: whole sections of it are covered by a thick layer of rotting algae.

"*Spirogyra*," says Igor as Kenshij gathers a handful of it and lifts it to his nose. "It came along when industries started discharging into the Selenga, Angara and Barguzin rivers. The water was poisoned, and the subsequent eutrophication made it unusable for people and animals. In the summer it takes superhuman effort to clean a part of the beach. You have to dig down at least thirty centimeters to get rid of it. Fishing has become impossible too. The boats can't move, they can't cast their nets because of the banks of algae floating on the surface."

Huge shards of ice, like sharp, white, ragged fangs, sparkle on the lake. Miriam points to somewhere far off. "And those down there?"

"Purifiers . . . installed along the Selenga to limit the pollution from the paper factories, including the BAIKALSK

Pulp and Paper Mill. Luckily, it closed down in 2013. It didn't do much good though, and they couldn't keep up with the urban discharge and the nitrates being washed off the cultivated land."

Stinking heaps of decomposing algae spread for kilometers along the beaches; the littoral is paved with a hectacomb of dead fish sticking out of the ice, with tufts of unyielding yellowish algae that can survive the -20°C or -30°C temperatures,; spongy blobs covered with reddish streaks, the colors of an irreversible disease.

"There used to be a miniscule crustacean that kept it all clean, filtering the water until it was crystal clear. There also used to be a kind of plankton that many species fed on, but as soon as the salinity changed, oxygen levels diminished and the temperature rose, and the shrimp died out within the space of ten years. This was the only place it lived, it was an endemic species, unable to survive anywhere else."

On the hill, the monument in honor of Marina Rikhvanova, president of the Baikal Ecological Wave organization, who successfully mobilized environmental associations, sensitized institutions and convinced the government in Moscow to deviate the course of the gas pipeline from the banks of the lake, has been covered with black paint. Someone has covered the eyes of the ten-meter-high statue placed with arms open to the sky at the start of the Great Baikal Trail, a well-equipped footpath circumnavigating the lake. It is hard to say whether it was an act of senseless vandalism or of pity, to stop her from seeing what has been happening in her absence.

"As if that wasn't enough," Igor goes on, "in the last twenty years, three hydroelectric stations have been built along the Angara: Bratsk, Irkutsk and Ust-Ilimsk. The fourth station, in Boguchansky, is in the design phase."

A group of twenty ice skaters speed past thirty meters from them. Then they see a group of fifty snow bikess with wide tires ride past, and then a bunch of runners in bright tack suits training for the marathon.

"How can they ignore all this pain?"

"Tourists don't come here anymore . . . The athletes, on the other hand, ignore everything."

As they move beyond an inlet they come across an expanse of cadavers. Their entrance to a cemetery of molluscs, snails and shells is announced by the sound of empty shells crunching beneath their feet. Kenshij can't hide his horror. He lets them know that he wants to leave.

Then, in a weak voice he says, "When you walk along a path, part of the path enters you." Miriam turns because it is very rare to hear his voice. "Every touch is an exchange with the world. Today we are dead," he ends in a gloomy voice.

"Igor," says Miriam, taking him by the arm, "we have to ask the mayor to call a citizens' assembly."

The Church of the Icon of the Mother of God

All the inhabitants of Khuzhir are gathered in front of the Church of the Icon of the Mother of God. There are also some people on the other side of the fence watching the meeting.

It is very cold, and they are sipping tea and hot drinks from thermos flasks.

". . . And the scientists from the Limnology Institute of the Academy of Science and representatives from the Ministry of Natural Resources of Irkutsk, who have been to study the situation in recent years, haven't managed to fix much. The consequences of the proliferation of the algae are evident. We have to react!" Igor says at the end of his speech.

Public assemblies usually unfold in an atmosphere of tension. Those times are gone, along with the population who has moved elsewhere.

The only representative from the environmental associations highlights that it is the regional government's responsibility to develop a plan for the construction and modernization of wastewater treatment plants, and for the Baikalsk power station too. The dismantling and decontamination of the old BPPM paper mills and lignin residues falls to the regional government too, if not the federal one.

Murmurs of approval. Some grimaces. Some clapping.

A young lady starts to speak. Her features are smooth, with elongated eyes and a slender nose, as if she had been sculpted by the weather over the course of millennia. She is holding a baby in her arms, and has another in a stroller, "If the lignin reaches the Irkut river, it can reach further down. RG-GEOLOGY possesses 500 hectares of land near Moty and the vice director, Gleb Ivanov, guaranteed that our district would remain lignin free. According to the agreement signed five years ago, refusals can only be taken to specialized dumps, but the land around Moty isn't a dump. He promised to provide a list of places suitable for this material. What happened to it?"

The problem is huge: up to eight million cubic meters of lignin mud are still buried in the industrial trenches and in the sedimentation basins of the Solzansky and Babkhinskiy dumps along the coast.

Miriam watches impotently at this passing on of responsibility. Kenshij, on the other hand, makes a gesture with his chin to indicate to the cars with the darkened windows parked near the church. Without standing out, he gets up and goes to check. When he comes back, he shows her a picture on his phone.

"Mongolian plates," she whispers, "the guys from the dam Igor mentioned."

In the meantime, an old man is losing himself in tales of when Lake Baikal was a spectacle of nature.

"My grandfather used to take me fishing for *omul* . . . as soon as they were pulled up, they would scream like crows. Oh, there used to be so many strange things. With school friends we would dive to see the 'Baikal horses,' a crustacean that held on to stones in its pincers . . . perhaps to help it sink and rise."

This started a competition of who could tell the most nostalgic stories.

"One time I caught an eighty-kilo sturgeon that was carrying almost six kilos of caviar in its body!" Says an ex-fisherman who now runs the Revyakin town museum, which exhibits bits and pieces from the twentieth century. His overcoat is in itself a display of medals and badges from the now-defunct red army.

"Does anyone remember the transparent, oily *goljanki*?" Asks a *babushka* wearing a fake fur and a typical Buryat patterned scarf. "The females would give birth to two thousand babies ready to swim, and after all that effort died and floated to the surface. The pressure down there in the deep is so high that when they came to the surface they exploded, leaving oil slicks full of vitamin A all over the lake. My mother used to collect it for the house lamps."

Mayor Nikolai Šelichov is standing to one side as if all this has nothing to do with him. Every now and then he sends a voice message, receives a text, nods approval to this or the other person and shakes the hand of anyone who comes to greet him.

The meeting is heading up a blind alley.

Igor, all agitated, moves closer to Miriam and Kenshij. "I get it now! Šelichov and the other mayors are letting the Baikal rot to lower land prices and force people out, then they can sell everything off to the multinationals running the Mongolian dam. In the case of a disaster, they won't have to pay anyone compensation." Then he gestures towards the girl who had complained earlier. "How long do you think Ajuna Lebedeva can hold out with two children and a degree in engineering, forced to print 3D souvenirs for the ghosts of tourists?"

Miriam's heart breaks and she can think of nothing to say. Instead, her attention is caught by the Church of the Icon of the Mother of God, with its sky blue roof and the onion-shaped domes typical of orthodox architecture. Despite this, the materials look shiny and artificial.

"When was the church built?"

"Oh that . . . it is really recent. Sometimes the *Sarma* blows for days, it can be so strong that it uproots trees, capsizes boats and rips roofs off houses. Last year it took the old church away . . . Around here there used to be an antique tradition of building *obydennye cerkvi*, little chapels erected in a day thanks to the efforts of all the members of a community. It was a symbol of collaboration, a solid example of a Russian 'miracle': a church built in the present where before there were only trees, a space to get to know each other through the contributions of everybody."

"But you said that it is a really recent construction."

"Yes, because a week after the storm, a group of volunteers and friends of Ajuna launched an online petition and within twenty-four hours they found themselves with enough money to reprint it, identical to the previous one. This time, though, the roof has been anchored to the land," Igor finishes, pointing out the supports, like buttresses.

"That means there are hidden energies, they are just dispersed and neutralized by something or someone pushing against them . . ."

Kenshij casts a sideways look at the mayor.

"Exactly," says Miriam. "We will never be able to make him change his mind. For him, what he can't see or understand, does not exist. But with a little imagination the others could get there."

Uros

Together with Sasha and Lena in the double stroller, Ajuna Lebedeva waves at Miriam from a distance. Tanja and Lev do the same, her friends from university.

Miriam throws a ball into the air and does a few dives and somersaults and catches it before it hits the ground. At seventy-nine, she playssports as well as her morning Qi Gong exercises with Kenshij. Her grey hair blows backwards and forwards in the breeze. Her body is flexible and toned.

"Hello everyone! Come on, we were waiting for you," says Miriam, welcoming the group into the space between the tents composed a few days earlier. After filling each of their flasks with an infusion of redcurrant and raspberry, she leads the way to the back of their camp.

Kenshij and Igor are positioned at either side of a table holding a basin full of water.

"We wanted to show you something, we will obviously need help. The plan for getting the Baikal back is made up of two stages, without the first we won't be able to go ahead with the second."

Behind them, two nanomats are composing some five-by-five centimeter brown cubes, a third is extruding a greenish elastic filament, and the last is depositing layers of the same material in one-centimeter-thick sheets.

Excited, Sasha and Lena wave their hands around because they want to play with these bizarre objects.

"A long time ago I used to live in Rome, and in that life I worked for twenty years for the World Food Program as a nutritional analyst. One time we went on a mission to Peru, to Lake Titicaca, to study the nutrition habits of the Uros, a population of the Andes that has adapted to a hostile environment. They make use of the few resources available to them. Most of all, an aquatic plant similar to rushes, known as *totora*, is the basis of their survival; the Uros use it to build boats and homes and they use the white part of the cane as a hangover cure. The sprouts can be eaten, and the flowers are used to make tea. Dried *totora* is good for burning for heating and cooking, and as a material for braiding souvenirs. We will do the same with the *Spirogyra*."

Ajuna pulls out her phone and starts to record.

Kenshij takes a handful of cubes and passes them to Igor, who wraps them, one by one, in the green filament. To the delight of Sasha and Lena two cubes end up in their hands.

"Our hated alga is going to be transformed into bricks of mud and peat designed with miniscule bubbles of oxygen trapped inside them so they can float."

Once the cubes are tied together with the filament, Igor puts them in the basin and they all watch as they float, half submerged, half bobbing on the surface of the water. Then Kenshij and Igor take some of the sheets of algae still hot from printing, and lay them out on the floating platform.

"Once we have printed hundreds of blocks, we will have the foundations on which we can place many layers of *Spirogyra* sheets to make a kind of floor. As the layers get worn out and crumble because of decomposition caused by the underwater bacteria, we will only have to add new layers over the top to keep everything compact from one year to the next."

Ajuna is speechless, the idea is so simple she can hardly believe it will work.

"Do you want to compose yurts, tents and buildings on there?"

"Yes, with some care it is entirely possible."

"With time, the blocks will grow together to form a single living layer that can be connected to a nearby island or fixed to the bottom of the lake with stone anchors. Braided *Spirogyra* will create a spongy surface, dry and elastic, two meters thick. You'll be able to run and dance on it!"

Ajuna's dark, penetrating eyes stare at the little model. She can see a future that was unthinkable a few minutes ago; thoughts of her house being threatened by the lignin deposits in Moty vanish, and she imagines her children running around with other children, swimming in the lake full of fish and looking after that wondrous place that tourists will come from half the world to see and admire. Then she comes back to reality and swaps a perplexed look with Tanja and Lev.

"It won't be easy to convince whole villages to gather *Spirogyra*," Ajuna says, expressing her doubts, based on past experiences. "They have seen it grow and spread like a cancer. They have ripped it, attacked it with acid and weed killers, they have even tried burning it, like they used to do with witches."

Miriam calls a Siberian cat to her with a gesture, its fur is long and white, and it has been stalking around the area since they set up camp.

"You're right, but if this idea manages to plant a seed, we will be able to make it so the seedlings will sprout in other places too."

Ajuna is sharing the film clip she made with Tanja and Lev so they can launch it on the social networks.

"Actually it might not be so hard," Igor interjects, reanimated by a charge that up until a few days ago was desperation. "The people of the villages around here, right up to Kransojarsk, Irkutsk and Magadan, are fed up of hearing the same old promises about cleaning up the Baikal that are never kept, and those preposterous ones about heating Siberia with nuclear energy, melting the permafrost to feed the power stations . . . How many have we heard?"

Lev adds his thoughts, "You're right, they had us signing petitions to irradiate the Arctic cities with artificial sunlight."

"People want food to eat without too much effort," Tanja agrees. "I had my own farm, but between the climate going crazy and environmental disasters, it has become difficult here, you might even say dangerous for our health."

Miriam and Kenshij share a look of complicity. Perhaps this generation is ready, more out of necessity than choice, to take the big step, the same one they took when they freed themselves from industrial nutrition.

"Do you know about nanites?"

"I've read some stuff in scientific magazines," Ajuna says, "and in science fiction novels."

"Well, they are like artificial genes equipped with motors to be able to move: a gyroscope, a growth battery, a calibration system, a cellular membrane sensor and a manipulator. Then there are parts I never can remember . . ." Miriam pauses, trying to remember the terms, ". . . a wavelength sensor, organized logic circuits, an anti-receptor of T cells and an emergency-destruct system."

"What do they do that is different from normal genes?"

"The ones we have allow us to lower our nutritional needs by 80%. Where before we ate two or three times a day, we now eat two or three times a month."

The kids can't help laughing.

"Do you have to go to the bathroom?" Tanja asks, blushing.

"Rarely, but yes, we do, we are just more efficient. The less that goes in, the less there is to come out."

"Now I remember, I saw something about this on the internet," says Tanja. "You are the PULLDOGS, you started the *walkersways* in the north!"

"Exactly, Igor called us here to help."

At this point Ajuna is convinced and wants to know everything; she takes a cube out of Lena's hands and looks at it carefully, "And what is the second part?"

"It's even more complex, but I can explain it to you."

LOSERS'S HAPPINESS

Lying on the snow under the stars, arms folded behind their heads and eyes closed, Miriam, Kenshij and Igor are listening to the Baikal. The *Sarma* is making a line of trees sway, freeing a scattering of chromed leaves.

"These are . . . poplars," she says, recognizing the trees' rustling.

Igor can't believe it; he doesn't believe her and opens is eyes to check. Amidst the branches something incredible is taking shape.

"What are those? Nanites?"

"No, strengthened pollen, nanites are invisible. But they are beginning make their presence felt."

Banks of spores fluctuate through the air, pushed along by the nocturnal breeze, very fine granules with artificial bioluminescence; the night shatters into myriad shards, sparkling drops expelled vigorously by the trees. Above their heads, the breezes carry the perfume of resin and birch trees: a shipwreck of inflorescence, waves of transparent rarefied mucilage over the surface of the Baikal.

Sniffing isn't enough: Igor raises his arms and lets a bank of spores brush his skin, penetrating the fractal geometries. He feels like the whole of science if passing through him, the beauty and infinite wisdom enclosed by the forests.

"Will we be able to communicate with them one day?"
He asks, almost in a trance.

"They are already talking and communicating with us, using perfumes and chemical substances . . ."

"But perhaps nanites will become the interpreters of these unknown languages."

Three months have passed since they arrived and the first changes in the people and the land are becoming visible. Miriam's words, NANITES FOR EVERYBODY, have had the same impact as a revolutionary slogan: where on one hand "for everybody" was easy to understand in a lawless land that hadn't forgotten communism, on the other hand the phrase was almost incomprehensible for many people since "nanite" refers to something invisible, like a gene, which in reality, incorporates characteristics linked to culture and the typical behavior of the meme. A meme acts like a grapevine, like a story propagating from person to person because it works.

One day Ajuna, Tanja and Lev, together with the people left in the village, took the snowmobiles, and at about five hundred meters from the shore, made a hole in the ice using ten hand drills. Then they began "terraforming" the Baikal, inserting about a hundred *Spirogyra* blocks and an equal number of pre-printed sheets of algae from home.

The seeds of the platform had been sown and the mayor wouldn't notice a thing. At most, the reconnaissance drones would mistake them for fishermen, desperately hunting for fish. Nevertheless, in the spring there would be a shoot pushing up through the broken ice sheet—something incredible would be sprouting, brick after brick, to transform into a refuge for families escaping from their lands and the consequences of the environmental disaster.

At that point, in the space of a few weeks, inertia would change, and having already composed the rest of the material during the winter months, it would be enough to transport it to the lake, put the pieces together and baptize the floating village. The first residential nucleus would house a dozen or so families in yurts, a hydroponic farm, an enclosure for fish, Ajuna's Fab Lab, a nursery for the small children and a lookout tower with an antenna for internet, all on one living infrastructure. It would be the attraction of the Baikal, a motive to return for the people who had had to leave its polluted shores unwillingly.

Miriam stands and notice lights coming from the lake.

-... ..- --- -. .- -. --- -- .

She goes into the tent to get her solar torch, switches it on and answers with the same sequence, "Goodnight to you too."

EPISCHURA BAIKALENSIS

The first caravans have started coming down from the hills.

The induction-driven solar sleds slide lightly, twenty centimeters above the snow.

"Watch the show, my friend. The reinforcements are coming to decolonize the future."

Waving their arms, Miriam and Kenshij greet the traveling communities of Neotopia, Wanderworld and Noburgh. Their presence, in addition to the composition of the archipelago, would be really helpful in the event that the mayor thinks up some kind of cunning plan or disturbance activity.

From the opposite side, Ajuna's friends emerge from the woodland, escorted by some Caucasus shepherds as if they were the *Lešie* of Slavic legend, forest dwelling spirits, protectors of the territory who emanate mysterious energy. They grab freshly printed shovels, pitchforks and rakes for clearing the beach and gathering *Spirogyra*.

Kenshij runs to help them and Ajuna moves over to Miriam and entrusts her with a jewellery box decorated with the red and blue patterns of Mongolian Buddhism.

"We had to move around a lot to find it, from Irkutsk to Seleginsk, right up to Ulan-Ude, luckily there was still a specimen in the Listvyanka museum. To begin with, the man in charge tried to put us off, like always, and we had to go back with old Kolya from our museum in Revyakin. In the end, with his help, they gave it to us."

"Good, we will take it back as soon as we can. All we need is a sample."

Sleeping in the box is a specimen of the famous Baikal shrimp, waiting to be reawoken. It is a tiny creature, just 2 millimeters long. At one time these made up 90% of the lake's biomass and were the first block in the food chain for the *golomyanka*, which in turn fed the *nerpa*, the only freshwater seal in the world.

Once they have a sample of DNA from the preserved creature, all they have to do is inject the genetic material into the egg sacks of the shrimp species most closely related to the extinct one, the *Heterocope septentrionalis*. The crustaceans cloned in this way would have a high probability of surviving and recreating the *Epischura baikalensis*. Additionally, the insertion of nanites will accelerate the process of engineering the desired traits.

"The Baikal cleaner will be back, ready to make the water clear again."

Igor leaves his tent wrapped in a blanket. He is feverish and overtaken by shivering caused by having taken nanites. It will take weeks before his organism adapts to the mutation and re-establishes a metabolic balance. In the meantime, his adhesion to the PULLDOGS is complete: for him, ecolution has become the perfect synthesis of mysticism and pragmatism, a kind of spiritual engineering worthy of the cosmists of yesteryear. He says he will save a piece of Russia and harmonize a strip of the world because, in the emptiness left by communism and capitalism, there must be space for an ideology aiming to reconcile the desire for personal liberty and a sober and aware lifestyle.

His eyes are red, his face is swollen, but his eyes are bright.

"I don't know how to thank you, Miriam. You have snapped us all out of our stupid beliefs. You have gathered every strand of our hidden energy. You have given us back the Baikal, not only to the Buryat, but to anyone else who wants to visit or live here."

"And I thank you too, Igor Mikhailovic. It would have been easier to give up, surrender to desperation, let yourself drift and die out like the poor shrimp. But here you are, with a fever that is electrifying you."

"I would like the mayor to see what we have seen."

Miriam turns and points up, towards Khuzhir.

"Then say hello to him, he is watching us. His drones are up there. He has never stopped watching us."

Igor blinks. Between the branches of the trees, they can just make out two hovering shapes. Something snaps inside him. He takes off the blanket and starts running half naked towards the drones. His feet sinking up to the ankles in the snow.

"Don't you get it yet?" He shouts like a madman at the drone. "You have to let go of some of the control to get a little balance in return!" He drops to the ground, hands in the snow, and picks up a couple of stones. "You have to stop drawing a line between us and the rest of the world!"

He throws the stones and misses the target but perhaps achieves his goal, then he falls to his knees, dropping to the ground exhausted. Miriam and Ajuna go to him and put a blanket over him.

"Damn him and all those like him. They force us to obey, put up with tragedies, ask for forgiveness for our weaknesses, accept the most inhuman and unnatural habits, in order to do no more than survive."

The wind calms down. The still air is icy. The drones float beyond the hill.

"Igor, listen to me," says Miriam, resting her warm hands on his face. "The floating islands will not be like those canvas and cardboard villages Prince Potemkin had built when Catherine the Great was passing through. We won't be trying to fool anyone—least of all ourselves—into believing we have the solution in our hands. We expect further battles. The plans for the dam won't be abandoned because we have started cleaning the lake. Pëtr Alekseevič Kropotkin, one of my son Alan's favorite thinkers, once wrote, "We will reach Arcadia through Anarchy."

The first floating residents are gathered on a soft floor of algae under the Fab Lab HOUSE OF CREATIVITY sign.

The nanomats are working on a continuous cycle, twelve sets of 3D printers are connected to about twenty matter reservoirs (made of biodegradable fiber and resin) from which they take the necessary quantities, following open-source formulas from the E-DEN online archives.

Today is a special day, a day of celebrations, but also of farewells.

Vibrations start rising from the throats of Ajuna, Tanja, Lev and other friends who have come to say goodbye to Miriam and Kenshij.

For the Tuva people, Xöömej throat singing is a sound continuum that evokes nature's elementary forces: water, air and earth. The tongue, touching the roof of the mouth, separates the throat and mouth into two different sound boxes, producing a monody of a disquieting purity.

With closed eyes, the faces of the singers unite in a single vibrating expression.

At the beginning, the single notes spread in slow metallic modulations, no vibrato, almost as if they are whispering flutes. Then, all of a sudden, they break and separate with dramatic effect, the notes dropping in tone and becoming really low. No instrument exists that is capable of producing a similar strange effect. They all have their eyes closed, enraptured by the divine frequencies.

It is an experience that goes beyond music: it is a sense of a lost place, the Baikal, and fully incarnates its sacredness. These voices, the Shamanka Rock, these are the lake's sanctuaries.

At the end of the song, Miriam is tearing up and even Kenshij is finding it hard to keep back the tears.

"How wonderful . . . What can I say? Adopt the slow, patient gait of nature to grow together with that which is not human, flower in every new season, learn from each other; the challenge is to learn to listen stories that are different from our own to help them develop alongside us. Our paths are separating," Miriam says solemnly, "but everything paths divide, paths reunite."

The children run to greet the walkers. Miriam and Kenshij gather them into their arms and hug them: their sorrow at departing is mitigated by the joy of having known these people and the memories of them they will keep inside on the long trek along the *walkersways* during the spring. The times to go and come back are no longer as clear as they used to be.

Igor is ready too, to build, fight and defend: the first mutation is about to come to an end and he can't wait to put his new anatomy to the test, wearing t-shirts and shorts.

Miriam takes a basket of fresh produce from Ajuna's hands—blackberries, raspberries, and redcurrants—just before they get on the jet ski that will take them to land.

"According to the legend," Ajuna says, "Lake Baikal had a daughter, Angara, who fell in love with a young man called Eniseja and they ran away together. Baikal didn't want to let them go, and, to stop the two lovers, threw the shaman's stone at them. Today this is known as Shamanka Rock, which is also considered the source of the Angara River. You have done the same, you have stopped many families from running from here by throwing these islands into the middle of the lake. Every time you want to come to visit us, you can camp in the cave; that is your place."

From a distance they can hear the hissing, like whistling, made by the lake birds returning to the shores of the Baikal. Kenshij had seen some of these over the past few months, but it is only now, in spring, that shy flocks of black storks and partridges from the steppes are beginning to reappear on their hunt for a seasonal nesting ground.

Everybody turns to see them glide in.

"Who knows where they will nest," says Ajuna. "When they used to nest at the level of the lake, it meant the summer would be arid and if they nested in the tops of the trees, it meant it would probably be rainy."

"From now on," says Miriam, climbing onto the jet ski with Kenshij, "you can admire them without worrying about where they are nesting. Ecolution will protect you from drought and flooding, it will allow you to adapt to the mutability of the seasons, you will float with the environment, you will be an integral part of it, there will no longer be any reasons to have to run away."

Revivalist or specialist in de-extinction: At the speed with which flora and fauna species have been disappearing over recent years, the zoologists and botanists of today could play a fundamental role in bringing extinct species back to life, re-integrating new species directly into the natural habitats of their predecessors. In view of a possible environmental catastrophe or a rapid, inexorable loss of biodiversity, a seed bank has been built on the Norwegian Svalbaard Islands. Perhaps it would be worth doing the same thing for animals, a kind of ark for the future, ready to face an apocalypse.

Re-forestry rangers: With a background in botany and natural sciences, the re-forestry rangers would have the task of transforming a concrete jungle into a green belt. Furthermore, anyone with a specialization in industrial archaeology and/or urban architecture, could decide which industrial ruins and landscapes to preserve and which to remove, replacing abandoned factories, obsolete buildings, disused roads and useless infrastructures with forests and native species.

Vertical agriculture: It is estimated that by 2050, without radical modifications to our present food production and consumption system, it will be necessary to have the resources of another two planets to feed the world's population. The vertical farm worker will be involved with the urban cultivation of plants and vegetables, resorting to both aeroponics and hydroponics, drastically reducing the level of land needed, the consumption of water and the transport of raw materials. Every building composed of numerous living units could aim for local nutritional sustainability by cultivating urban kitchen gardens, and, on the vertical structures, everything the apartment block needs. A further future development could be zero gravity agriculture, in sub-orbital factories and lunar settlements.

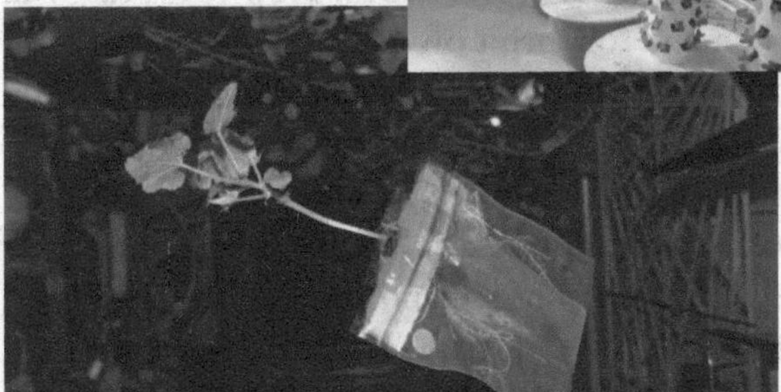

Renewable energy and circular economy consultant: It is, by now, certain that the use of fossil fuels cannot continue much longer. An alternative energy consultant is a specialist, an expert in all types of renewable energy sources: solar, hydroelectricity, geothermal, wave power and biomass. According to specific needs, the expert can advise which energy source would be the best fit, collaborating on the creation of the best solution to reach off-grid energy independence and autonomy.

Repairer/Creator of organ parts: 3D printers could revolutionize the healthcare sector, and together with the progress in stem cell research could, within a few years, cause an exponential demand for "print on demand" organs. In addition to healthcare, it is possible it could be useful in other areas such as sports and plastic surgery. As the cost of this kind of printing decreases, access to this type of personalized supply of organs could be available to a large number of people. Like with "print on demand" books, the same is on the cards for organs.

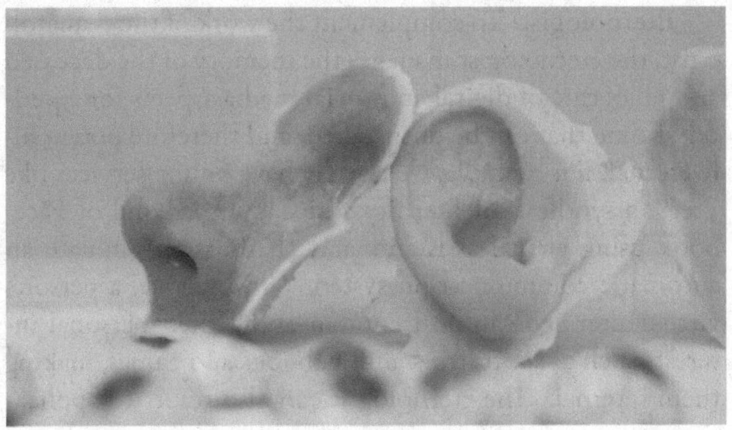

Digital thanatology: Currently, Facebook is the largest digital cemetery that has ever existed. It has over fifty thousand profiles of users who have died and continues to see about 33,000 deaths per day (out of a total of 151,600 deaths daily throughout the world in 2011).[30] The digital death manager will organize the period preceding death, taking care of a digital will and other bequests, as well as the following stage through the management of social media profiles, virtual relationships and possibly using automatic chatbots, with the aim of softening the pain of loss and helping with the process of mourning for anybody who knew the user. Following this, and depending on a person's last wishes, the DDM could de-index the deceased's presence from web contents, hide it from search engines, or even delete it definitively. Vice versa, they can maintain a user's memory thereby restoring them to their living contacts through posts, messages, shares and comments.

---

30 Davide Sisto, La morte si fa social, Bollati Boringhieri, 2018, pag. 71; Cfr. http://www.ecology.com/birth-death-rates/.

Eternologist: To complement the work of the thanatologist, the eternologist manages the memory of the deceased and takes care of digital and social media aspects for a period of time that can be unspecified, and therefore potentially eternal. For example, we already have online services like Eter9, a synthesis of Eternity and Cloud9, a kind of Facebook using virtual assistants and chatbots to simulate an automatic communication system.[31] In practice, a person's virtual alter ego can post content about their personal interests such as sport, trips, music, books and games, making them "eternal." The eternologist can also resort to applications such as LifeNaut, with which they can create digital clones of human beings capable of simulating the presence of the deceased. Mindfile (an electronic backup of someone's personality) and a Buiofile (cryogenic record of someone's DNA) prepare us for future resurrection, when technology is at a stage where this is possible. In the meantime, the eternologist can continue to have the deceased appear in the shape of an avatar or a hologram and have them integrate with friends and relatives on special occasions or birthdays, and, who knows, allow them to make important decisions from the afterlife.

3D food engineer: The world population will reach nine billion by 2050. Current agricultural systems will no longer be capable of providing enough food for everyone. Food cultivated in laboratories and even that from 3D printers is destined to become part of our diet.

Drone traffic controller: Today we already use drones to shoot film for us, fight our wars for us, perform surveillance of our neighborhoods and deliver our goods—these are the

---

31 Eter9, https://www.eter9.com/auth/login.

intentions, at least. In a few decades, they will be all over the place. There will have to be someone tracking their flight paths, so they do not cause damage or traffic in low altitude urban airspace.

Bibliography

Solarpunk: Histórias ecológicas e fantásticas em um mundo sustentável edited by Gerson Lodi-Riberio (Draco, 2012)

Solarpunk: Ecological and Fantastical Stories in a Sustainable World (World Weaver Press, 2018)

Sunvault: Stories of Solarpunk and Eco-Speculation, edited by Phoebe Wagner and Brontë Christopher Wieland (Upper Rubber Boot, 2017)

Eco-Punk, Speculative Tales of Radical Futures, edited by Liz Grzyb and Cat Sparks (Ticonderoga Publications, 2017)

Glass and Gardens: Solarpunk Summers, edited by Sarena Ulibarri (World Weaver Press, 2018).

Pacific's Edge, Kim Stanley Robinson, Orb Books, 1990

La parabola del seminatore, Octavia Butler, Solaria n.4, Fanucci, 2000

New York 2140, Kim Stanley Robinson, Fanucci 2017.

Biketopia: Feminist Bicycle Science Fiction Stories in Extreme Futures, edited by Elly Blue, Microcosm Publishing, 2017

Ecotopia, Ernest Callenbach, Bantham, 1975

The Weight of Light, edited by Clark A. Miller, Center for Science and the Imagination, Arizona State University, 2019

A Golden Thread, 2500 Years of Solar Architecture and Technology, Marion Boyars Publishers, 1981.

Linkography

Adam Flynn, Solarpunk: Notes toward a Manifesto https://hieroglyph.asu.edu/2014/09/solarpunk-notes-toward-a-manifesto/

Medium: https://medium.com/solarpunks

Solarpunk Anarchist: https://solarpunkanarchists.com/

Elvia Wilk, Is ornamenting Solar Panels a crime? https://www.e-flux.com/architecture/positions/191258/is-ornamenting-solar-panels-a-crime/

Interview with Adam Flynn: https://solarpunkcity.com/2017/11/24/the-godfather-of-solarpunk-interviewed-adam-flynn/

Interview with Gerson Lodi-Ribeiro: https://solarpunkcity.com/2017/05/31/solarpunks-interviewed-gerson-lodi-ribeiro/

At the Very Least We Know the End of the World Will Have a Bright Side: https://longreads.com/2018/12/12/solarpunk-review/

What is solarpunk? https://solarpunkanarchists.com/2016/05/27/what-is-solarpunk/

How Green the City Is

by Clelia Farris

Science fiction has a preference for setting stories in large cities, overcrowded and chaotic. It's no coincidence that one of the first science fiction films was called *Metropolis*. When it came out in the 1920s, the world population was in the process of migrating from rural areas to towns and cities, and the trend, as the economists say, is still growing. By 2050, 70% of the world population will be living in cities.

All the main characters in the stories in *Ecolution* live in Rome, which is gradually becoming the *Caput Fantascientiae* (the center of science fiction). Carla and Basma live in a community in the city outskirts. Elisa suffers inside a shopping center, the name of which—Porta di Roma—defines the location. The anonymous protagonist of "Greenglimmer" lives in an anonymous residential neighborhood. Shi comes from Rome and travels to see her father who lives in a heavily technological Chinese village that has lost any signs of its rurality. Miriam also comes from Rome, her path leading her all the way to Siberia.

Each find themselves dealing with the disturbing animal that the city is, a creature that requires them to live according to its hierarchical and centralizing structure. The urban agglomerate is an organism made up of specialized areas: it has a brain (local government), a circulatory system (the streets), lungs (parks and gardens) and a digestive tract (the sewers). Like an animal, the city cannot do without any of its systems, and it is this weakness the rebels' resistance relies on.

Adding a grain as small as a bird poop was enough to trip and definitively ruin the functioning of the shopping center, as in "The Nutators." After the guanopocalypse, this temple to consumerism empties of shops and customers to be re-populated with plants and animals. Its pace is no longer the hustle and bustle of compulsive buying, but the slow waltz of the nutation of the *Ailanthus* trees. A slowness also more suitable for human rhythms.

Then, it is sufficient to modify plants, render them capable of producing light and electricity to change the false urban jungle made up of aerials and electricity pylons disguised as trees, as in "Greenglimmer."

Each story in this anthology is an ecological solution to city problems. It is also a suggestion to "work with" rather than "work against" nature. In moments of crisis the human animal has always acted according to an escape plan. Temperatures are rising? Let's move north. Food is getting scarce? Let's change continents.

This behavior was successful while humanity lived in hunter-gatherer tribes. When it became sedentary and towns were established, it was necessary to change this adaptive response. Just like plants, cities cannot run. It is the time to risk new behaviors and it is more likely to be the people "on the edges" of a city who discard the usual responses in order to seek out innovative remedies to environmental mutations.

The residential outskirts, where the characters in these stories live, are also a reflection of their social standing. The most peripheral of them all are Billai and Haziz who come from Africa and are welcomed aboard the green ship, a utopian floating city sailing the Mediterranean. The green ship is an example of the perfect union between advanced technology and plants. A cosmos that is a precursor for metropolises of the future.

Carla and Basma live in a commune in the outskirts of Rome, an area suitable for cultivating kitchen gardens and energy independence. Colorado lives in Tufello, and it is there that he grows his "plant weapons." A thin green line linking the outskirts of the world, from Rome to the garden of Maestro Ming in China and to the shores of Lake Baikal in Siberia, confirms the fact that cities are also places of collective creativity, capable of innovating relationships between humans and the environment to create a diverse ecosystem.

The stories in *Ecolution* are profoundly solarpunk because, with a spirit of optimism and attention to bio-inspired engineering, they tell us that by following nature, or Tao, cities could evolve in a revolutionary manner, imitating plants, whose great strength consists of an absence of specialization. Plants are modular: each part of their organism carries out all the metabolic functions necessary for survival. No head, no stomach, no central control. If some of a tree's branches are attacked by fire, they can die without putting the whole plant at risk.

In some circumstances we too fall back on a kind of modularity. Much scientific, technical and literary knowledge is now recorded on servers, in the cloud and in the future, in robots. Stephan the android preserves the theory and practice of weaving byssus; Zhao the robot can embroider as well as the most expert old Chinese lady; the gynoid Jie records and memorizes the traditional songs of the Miao people.

Androids possess all the characteristics humans do, shape and thought, in a near-immortal enhanced frame. Trusting complex functions to external systems seems normal to us, even more so if the external module looks just like us. However, we have not yet managed to plan the human environment in such a way as to copy the vitality of a forest.

Cities are still developed according to "animal" criteria, specialization and concentration of function. We have reached the point where we build putting the economy, rather than human beings, first. The Porta di Roma neighborhood, as Colorado points out in "The Nutators," was built after the shopping center. The first thought is of commerce, and only after this is of consumers. Consumers, not citizens.

Specialization only has sense if the ecological niche remains stable. When everything changes, when the summers become torrid, the winters too cold and rain exaggerated, keeping parks separate from the living spaces is a contradiction.

Confining plants to certain sectors of a city does not eliminate heat bubbles, polluted air and social ills.

Urban suffering is the other uniting theme running through these stories. All the characters in *Ecolution* experience varying degrees of illness, from Elisa's Gruen syndrome, a form of allergy to synthetic substances, to the inhabitants of the area around Lake Baikal, poisoned by the algae that are prolific in polluted waters.

Urban structure has always been criticized as a source of anxiety, discomfort and discontent. The straight lines of the buildings, the sterility of the paving, the darkness of the asphalt, all work together to make the life of the city dweller less happy. The height of ecological ridiculousness is the "plastiplane trees" described in "Greenglimmer," electricity pylons disguised as trees, equipped with the capability of reproducing the sound of wind rustling non-existent leaves. It is these non-trees that provide the final straw for the protagonist who ends up seeking out an electricity-transmitting "plant" world.

Dissatisfaction with the environment has an important role in pushing the protagonists towards a different future using innovative solutions. Modified plants in "Greenglimmer," seed bombing in "The Nutators," nanite-enhanced pepper in "The Maestro of Small Things," hybrid shrimps that defeat the spread of algae in "Ecolution"; even on an island like Sant'Antioco, Carla and Basma manage to change the fate of Sa Giunchera and the *pinna nobilis* thanks to Stephan the android.

Environmental modification exists, it is happening. It is not a natural fact, or rather it is, by virtue of human beings being a part of nature and having acted in such a way as to choose a direction for the whole planet. A direction based on a political-economic system the entire planet subscribes to: capitalism. It is such a traumatic fact that we still find it difficult to be aware of it. Despite this, the heroes of these stories, in their modesty, do not let themselves be scared by what exists. For them, "growth" means roots in the ground, branches, leaves and flowers. "Progress" means purified water, workshops to learn weaving in and electric energy from plants.

In the end, existential discomfort is not a product of the city, but of the separation of the human environment from the natural environment. The stories in *Ecolution* allow us to imagine what would happen if the human/natural barrier were to fall, if our actions were to aim towards the construction of a shared future where plants, animals, human beings and biodiversity could be integrated to create an organic togetherness.

As in an alchemical transformation, the embers of the past burn slowly—plastic, steel, useless objects and ephemeral emotions all melt in the crucible of technological and spiritual renewal. From their ashes the alliance between animals, humans and nature will rise, and this will happen when all the desires of the past have been consumed.

Interview with Francesco Verso on Solarpunk, or rather, Solartivism

by Arielle Saiber

1) When and how did you start writing environmental science fiction (SF), particularly solarpunk?

My interest in environmental themes dates back to my university years in Amsterdam, where I studied Environmental Economics. It was one of the first programs available in Europe to explore the ambiguous relationship between economic systems and ecological consequences. My thesis was on "The Ecological Footprint of The Netherlands," showing how much material and immaterial overconsumption and externalities of the Dutch economy was dependent on importing cheap raw resources and exporting expensive high-tech goods. It created a high GDP balance that was hiding (or simply not accounting for) the real environmental costs of dumping pollution and waste on other countries. It is no surprise, then, that as soon as I started to write science fiction regularly, around 2004, those ideas were already well planted in my imagination. The first eco-fiction piece I wrote is called "Two Worlds," [*Due mondi*] a story (and a comic book) set in the far future, where two genetically engineered human species—the Aeromancers [Aeromanti] and the Aquamancers [Acquamanti]—must survive a radically transformed Earth that has been severely impacted by climate change. They embark on a quest to recover what remains of "the original seeds," which have been stored in a long-forgotten tower, which is the Global Seed Vault built on the Svalbard Islands in 2008.

Around 2017-18, I came across the subgenre of solarpunk while I was writing my two-volume novel *The Roam-*

ers. I found that solarpunk aligned perfectly with topics I was writing about in my fiction, such as a slow-paced "ecolution" [ecoluzione] of our lifestyle; a progressive embracing of "prosumerism"; and empowering non-privileged communities via peer-to-peer online barter, ubiquitous computing, radical food-intake reduction, off-grid solutions and a calculated degrowth to improve a general redistribution of wellness across different cultures using art and neo-nomadism. Over the years, I started to develop my own version of solarpunk which I call "solartivism," a mix of "solar + art + activism," or "solar + artivism."[32] Basically, solartivism is a way of using political activism to keep cutting-edge technologies free and accessible to as many people as possible. Its goal is to boost ingenuity by sharing good practices and incremental creativity.

2) How would you describe your style of solarpunk? How is it or isn't it aligned with other forms of clifi, eco-SF or optimistic SF?

I am interested in stories that question the status quo and propose a viable technological and economical alternative to our current system of living. My biopolitical narratives explore what lies outside and beyond the capitalistic and consumeristic reality. I try to do this in two ways:

• By writing my own speculative stories that are not strictly "hopeful" in the sense of wishful thinking—I personally consider hope to be a heteronomous force, which depends on external drives. I try to develop more of a sense of critical hope aimed at building practical and possible exit strategies to the actual dystopia proposed by the mainstream media as the new "normality" (or rather "abnormality"). I believe science fiction—and solarpunk in this specific context—should make the invisible visible;

---

32 More on Artivism: https://en.wikipedia.org/wiki/Artivism.

it should turn the impossible possible, allow the unimaginable to be imaginable, and represent its transformative message. It should be "ecolutionary."

• By giving voice to marginalized communities and cultures, untranslated languages, underrepresented traditions, unacknowledged native innovations and futures. I wish to bring to the table entities that have been and continue to be left out of the mainstream publishing sector and of the global science fiction conversation in English. These two obstacles keep dialogue fixed in a single global language, and they can be hypocritical in terms of inclusivity, as well as biased in their choice of technologies to represent in narrative. Their bulletproof copyrights can also be used as colonizing tools of neoliberalism and cyber-slavery.

My own vision for solarpunk, or rather, *"solartivismo,"* aims to de-carbonize, de-centralize, de-urbanize, de-patriarchalize and de-colonize the future.

3) Who (authors, artists, directors, etc.) are your primary inspirations for writing environmental SF?

The work of French thinker Serge Latouche on sustainable development and degrowth has been particularly enlightening in terms of imagining possible strategies out of the Western mindset. Spanish economist Joan Martinez Alier, who specializes in ecological economics and environmental justice, wrote a book entitled *Ecologies of the Poor*[33] that I think should be taught in high school and college. As it is nearly impossible to disentangle the ways we produce, transform, and dispose of resources and materials from how

---

33 Joan Martinez-Alier, *Ecology of the Poor: A Neglected Dimension of Latin American History,* Oxford University Press, 2004, https://www. jstor.org/stable/157387.

these actions impact the environment, I think we should no longer use the term "Anthropocene" to address our current climate crisis—it is a term often used and abused by the privileged. We should talk about "Capitalocene," as not all societies and production systems affect the environment in the same way, just as not all communities use/produce the same amount of energy, resources and waste.

Donna Haraway has been a great inspiration to me, with her focus on inclusivity and nonhuman agency. Her views on the importance of mingling with the "other" parallel the solarpunk view of a better society. Her *Staying with the Trouble: Making Kin in the Chthulucene* de-structures the pillars of contemporary Western society, introducing elements of interspecies collaborations and contaminations as the way to learn how to survive the wreckage of late capitalism.

When it comes to science fiction, I have found US writer Andrew Dana Hudson to have a particularly clear set of solarpunk ideas woven into his narratives. When I read Andrew's stories (I published his first collection of stories called *Lo stato solare* last year), I have the same "culture shock" I did when reading William Gibson's cyberpunk writing thirty years ago. His use of themes such as energy autonomy, resilient communities, inclusive policies, environmental sustainability and cooperation instead of competition envisions the next thirty to forty years with the same x-ray vision and cutting edge acumen as Gibson did in the 80s and 90s.

4) What are some of the major themes your solarpunk writing covers?

I am fascinated by the immense creativity of human cultures: indigenous innovation offers ingenious ways to solve critical issues such as nutrition, housing, education, healthcare and energy with what is available here and now: it *is* a kind of solarpunk. It can imagine and create long-term, sustainable ways of doing things locally, without shipping goods all over the world, damaging territories with alien commercial productions (like shrimp or palm trees) and imposing global standards to particular areas, like dislocating communities to create a park, a mall, a fast-fashion industry or livestock farm. Indigenous traditions know how to nurture cultural biodiversity, which can be used as a tool to oppose standardization, commodification and homogenization of views, ideas and, ultimately, futures. That is why I tend to connect my idea of solarpunk to a new "sense of wander," that is, a sense of moving through the world to find and cultivate neglected futures.

There was a time (from the 60s through the 80s of the last century) when important works of speculative fiction were translated from one country to another throughout the world, especially Europe, Russia, and Latin America. Today, however, the hegemony of English in the publishing world has created a situation in which every author wants to be translated into English, which then means that everyone knows everything about US and UK SF, while they completely ignore what is being written next door, for example between France and Germany, China and India, Brazil and Argentina and Russia and Finland. In reality, of course, high-quality science fiction is being written everywhere in every language; it is just that for most publishers, commercial concerns come first, so the readership does not necessarily end up with access to the best writing, but to the "best" books available in English. The cultural loss of such a short-sighted approach is huge. A study by the University of Rochester found out that only 3% of what is published in the US comes from a translation.[34] Similarly, on any SF shelf in any bookstore from Tokyo to Amsterdam, from Roma to Rio De Janeiro, there are hundreds and hundreds of books translated from English (a figure that in some markets goes up to 80%), and few from each nation's own writers or writers writing in languages other than English. That is what Antonio Gramsci would call a "cultural hegemony."

So, part of my contribution to solarpunk tries to dis-intermediate and disentangle SF from its dependency on the English language. In fact, as a literary genre, solarpunk emerged from Brasil around 2012, with the anthology "Solarpunk: Histórias ecológicas e fantásticas em um mundo sustentável" edited by Gerson Lodi-Riberio and developed in other major Latin American, African and subcontinent countries with different characteristics than the ones of the Northern hemisphere. In the Global South, solarpunk is trying hard to leverage ancient wisdom, traditional ways of practicing agriculture and sustainable methods of producing energy while reimagining their own native tools of innovation to regenerate the social and political tissue damaged by centuries of colonization and globalization.

Basically, I've asked myself: what would happen if we all read one single kind of story, experience one single kind of society, live in a single kind of economy and share one single view of the future? Solarpunk is indeed a global phenomenon and as such, it should include the voices and experiences of people speaking Portuguese, Arabic, Chinese, French, Spanish, Russian, Japanese and German, just to mention the most commonly spoken languages. Also, pretending that texts and stories should be "born in English" is imposing a

---

34 The 3% problem: http://www.rochester.edu/College/translation/threepercent/about/.

huge and unfair burden on all the people that do not speak English, many of whom do not have access to English language instruction and/or cannot afford to study it. There is a lot of work to do in this respect, not just on markets but mostly on the perception of reality.

For example, in my novel *The Roamers*, a group of people living in the twilight of Western civilization undergo an anthropological transformation caused by the dissemination of nanites (nanorobots capable of assembling molecules to create matter). This technology changes the way they eat: not three times a day, but once a month, which has an incredible impact on a person's food intake, food waste, ecological footprint, and income needs. This gives rise to a culture that, while reminiscent of an ancient nomadic society, is creative and new. The liberation from the "industry" of food, combined with the ability to 3D print one's own objects and tools and the use of open-access distributed cloud computing, makes it possible for these people to make a choice that would seem to us today almost impossible and anachronistic (although this choice might be closer to our present than we think). They give up their jobs, they start growing their own food and powering their own devices and they start walking outside of Rome. But the visions of the two main characters about how the newborn community should live collide, and so the group splits into two groups: one goes north to live in the beautiful wilderness of Siberia and Mongolia, while the other goes south to save the Dogon tribe from possible extinction due to climate change in Central Africa. In a near future that is in crisis over climate change and income inequality, the nomadic story of *The Walkers* brings a message of cultural and technological "ecolution" to our present world.

5) Is there anything particular about solarpunk produced in Italy, as opposed to what is being produced in other countries in Europe, Africa, Asia, the Americas and elsewhere?

From what I have read in Italian and in SF from the US and the UK, there is currently an abundance of stories focusing on a return to a simpler way of life: stories that offer a route to achieving a balanced relationship with nature and efforts to protect the environment and acquired social rights. This trend could be defined in broad terms as a new "cult of wilderness," a new kind of New Age (with fantasy and supernatural elements), a celebration of old wisdom as a necessary tool to preserve certain values threatened by modernity and techno-solutionism. In Italy, the US and the UK it advocates for a sort of return to an "arcadia." In Latin America, Africa and Asia, the focus is more on biopolitical discourse; property rights in both the material sense (land and water management) and the immaterial sense (copyrights and licensing); decolonizing the means of production, thereby removing these material and immaterial layers of globalization (e.g., climate injustice, negative externalities and secondary markets); and imagining their own futures, which have been cancelled, denied and ignored by centuries of colonialism, imperialism and late extractivism.

I could divide solarpunk into two kinds: 1) Solarpunk of the privileged, which can afford to optimistically imagine hopeful narratives that include cultivating past values of purity and innocence; and 2) Solarpunk of the non-privileged, which cannot look at the past without being horrified, and thus must turn to the future to build their identity and space of existence. For privileged narratives, the catastrophe is often, although not always of course, a thing of the *past*; it is behind them, it has already happened, and they are the ones who have survived it and must restart and rebuild a new civilization. For the non-privileged narratives, the catastrophe is happening now; it is in front of them and thus they must fight to overcome it, to create possible exit strategies to get away from the experience of daily apocalypses (a terrible job, lack of health care, denial of human rights, absence of education). When it comes to imagining futures, the privileged narratives do not often consider the present, but rather take the current dystopia for granted and continue to escape from the present as a sort of negation of the bad it cannot and will not face. The non-privileged narratives are forced to constantly look at the present and can only try to remove its presence as soon as possible in order to survive or succumb to it. The former can be driven by hope, the second is more often driven by desperation.

5) As an editor and publisher, what have you seen in terms of the reception to solarpunk (writing, art, media) in Italy?

There is a lot of interest in solarpunk in Italy, especially given that the last ten years of SF has been dominated by a self-replicating YA dystopia throughout the world. Big Italian publishers have not started publishing solarpunk, so it is, for now, a small press phenomenon. That said, agents in Italy have begun to say "no-more-dystopia-please," so it is possible that we'll see commercial publishers flooding the market with "solarpunkish" narratives soon.

The reception of solarpunk is very good, readers are willing to explore new narratives, both from a content and cultural point of view, embracing the multiple-futures POV shift that many people have been waiting for for a long time. And in doing so, I'm not trying to deny the dystopian present we all live in, I simply advocate a broader view of the future which includes other kinds of narratives, often less cynical and disillusioned ones.

My novel *The Roamers* has received excellent reviews on SF and literary websites by critics and readers and the anthologies "Solarpunk: come ho imparato ad amare il futuro" and "Solarpunk: dalla disperazione alla strategia" are among Future Fiction's best sellers at book fairs and conventions in Italy. I am often interviewed by radio stations, magazines and bloggers who want to know more about this new approach to Science Fiction, so I've also started to publish a small comic series dealing with solarpunk issues like "Two Worlds" [*Due mondi*] and "The Green Ship" [*La nave verde*] to bring these themes to a wider range of readers.

But it is not just a question of SF publishing. Solarpunk has garnered the interest of architects, artists, designers, urban planners and small community policy makers. There is a group of Italians living in the UK called "Commando Jugendstil" that is doing cool things with communication and illustrations, painting graffiti and murals in urban spaces.[35] They could be considered solarpunk street artists. Also, "Solarpunk Italia" is a website that has become, over the last two years, a sort of repository of articles, essays, videos and reviews in Italian about anything solarpunk happening in the world. Last summer, I organized a "Solarpunk Café" in collaboration with a group of researchers from the Faculty of Agriculture at the University of Pisa, where we had a conversation about the relationship between sustainable development, radical inclusivity, biopolitical decisions and urban planning.

---

35 https://cargocollective.com/mikeoloopie/Commando-Jugendstil.

6) Where do you see this kind of SF going? Do you predict that there will be more or less optimistic SF in the future?

One of the biggest risks I imagine is the normalization of solarpunk. That is, that it may become reduced to a meme, a trend, a hashtag, put on the shelves as a shiny cover or worn by a smiling model and displayed in the windows and sold like the dream of a happy future. I am afraid that what might happen with it will be similar to what happened with cyberpunk. In the words of William Gibson:

> *(...) I didn't have a manifesto. I had some discontent. It seemed to me that mid-century mainstream American science fiction had often been triumphalist and militaristic, a sort of folk propaganda for American exceptionalism. I was tired of America-as-the-future, the world as a white monoculture, the protagonist as a good guy from the middle class or above. I wanted there to be more elbow room. I wanted to make room for antiheroes.*[36]

Solarpunk could very easily be turned into a fashionable, commercial brand used to make money and exploit the "newness" of fake sustainability, inclusivity and solidarity. Capitalism thrives on the boredom of its disempowered consumers, and I foresee the risk that, if a sort of privileged, overexposed solarpunk overshadows the less-privileged ones—as has happened with the English language and SF in general—we will lose much of its power and activism.

There is nothing to be optimistic about if solarpunk will be "greenwashed" in the latest cool magazine, anthology or

---

36 William Gibson, The Art of Fiction No. 211," The Paris Review, 2011, https://www.theparisreview.org/interviews/6089/william-gibson-the-art-of-fiction-no-211-william-gibson.

convention, bending the original set of transformative global ideas into a trendy, exclusive, Burning Man-ish glittering experience, whether as a consolatory fantasy narrative with a hopeful ending, or as a winner-takes-it-all approach.

My work goes in the opposite direction, towards the creation of a network of small presses and authors collaborating to make SF intrinsically borderless, easily translatable, and widely replicable with the minimum amount of effort and money. Otherwise, it is not really solarpunk, but rather solarprank!

Bibliography

Hudson, Andrew Dana. *Lo stato solare*. Collecion of short stories. Ed. Francesco Verso. Rome: Future Fiction 2021.

Hunting, Eric. *Solarpunk: design ed estetica post-industriale*. Rome: Future Fiction, 2021.

________. *Multispecies Cities: Solarpunk Urban Futures*. Ed. Sarena Ulibarri, et al. Albuquerque: World
Weaver Press, 2021.

________. *Solarpunk: Histórias ecológicas e fantásticas em um mundo sustentável*, edited by Gerson Lodi-Riberio

________. *Sunvault: Stories of Solarpunk and Eco-speculation*. Ed. Phoebe Wagner and Brontë
Christopher Wieland. Nashville, TN: Upper Rubber Boot, 2017.

________. Glass and Gardens - Solarpunk Summers, edited by Sarena Ulibarri. Albuquerque: World Weaver Press, 2018.

________. Glass and Gardens - Solarpunk Winters, edited by Sarena Ulibarri. Albuquerque: World Weaver Press, 2020.

________. *Eco-punk!* Ed. Liz Grzyb and Cat Sparks. Greenwood, Western Australia: Ticonderoga
Publications, 2017.

Verso, Francesco. *I camminatori: Pulldogs*. Vol 1. Rome: Future Fiction, 2018.

________. *I camminatori: No/Mad/Land*. Vol. 2. Rome: Future Fiction, 2019.

________, ed. Francesco Verso. "Solarpunk. Dalla disperazione alla strategia."Rome: Future Fiction
2021.

________, ed. and Fabio Fernandes. *Solarpunk: Come ho imparato ad amare il futuro.*
Rome: Future Fiction, 2020.

Watson, Julia. *Lo Tek: Design by Radical Indigenism.* Taschen, 2019.

COMICS

Due mondi, Francesco Verso, Dark0 and 4Jinx and Cristina Tomasini, Futuresque series, Future Fiction, Roma, 2022

La nave verde, Francesco Verso, Gabriele Bitossi e Pietro Depalma, Futuresque series, Future Fiction, Roma, 2022.

Table of Contents

9 788832 077995